THE HOUSE THAT
ADELIA BUILT

by

MYA O'MALLEY

The House that Adelia Built

By Mya O'Malley
www.myaomalley.com

ISBN-13: 978-0-9978596-7-6
ISBN-10: 0-9978596-7-9

Cover Art by Jena Brignola
Formatting by Jill Sava, Love Affair With Fiction

FOR ALEXANDRA

PROLOGUE
1876

It was an evening like any other, yet it was to be a night that she would never forget—for it was a crucial piece of the puzzle that would ignite the course of Adelia's destiny.

Sharp, crisp wind bit at every inch of her exposed skin. Almost completely winded, Adelia spun her head once more, just to be sure she hadn't been followed here to the towering cliffs. A darkened sky matched her desperate, dismal mood.

Augustus never disappointed in stealing any smidgen of brightness from her mind, but tonight he had pushed until she too had crossed the thin line over to the brink of madness.

Yes, her husband was going mad.

Insane.

Insane with rage, jealously, control, apparently sparked by boredom and gin. Adelia couldn't imagine a worse possible combination. One could activate a fire sure to burn through and destroy any soul with those caustic ingredients.

Whenever Augustus would finally place his head on the pillow beside her, Adelia would wait out the thickness, the raw stench of alcohol and bitterness, until she could finally allow herself to breathe once Augustus began to snore. It was only then that her hands would grip the quilt, which rested upon her body. Then she would cautiously count to fifty. Fifty usually did the trick, but at times she had added a few seconds more, just to be sure.

Tonight, she had run for her life, not waiting for Augustus to pass out, leaving before his before his head had even hit the pillow.

Now safely outside, her fists unclenched and her breathing slowed until she could release the soft wail that fought to escape. As if she couldn't control it, her neck craned to spy behind her once more. Augustus had been at the gin for hours today, starting much earlier than ever before; she could only hope he wouldn't give chase, that he would pass out cold.

Recently, she had fooled herself into thinking that, if only she could try hard enough, perhaps they could get back to that sunny place where they had first fallen deeply for one another.

Was there such a spell? She frowned, knowing such a magic ceased to exist. Her trick no longer worked; she couldn't fool herself into thinking everything would be okay.

Not now.

Not anymore.

Months of self-reflection had consumed Adelia. She could hardly think of anything else. At first, she wondered if their downfall could have possibly been partly her own fault—Adelia may have played a hand at her heart's demise.

But, no, she had yet to find one shred of proof that argued against the fact that Augustus had been the one who had changed. Oh, it had been ever so slightly at first. An offbeat comment here and there, a sideways look. But after a few months, as surely as the dark tides shifted, it seemed that once they made the lighthouse on the cliffs their home, the very beacon which served to steer ships to safety in these treacherous waters diminished her own brightness and replaced it with a gradual shift to darkness.

She clung to the small sliver of a chance that she could fix this. Yes, she could throw her shoulders back and help this stranger her husband had shifted into, before it was too late.

Surely some came back from the brink of madness, right? But then the horrifying image that haunted her dreams plagued her mind once more. She shut her eyes tight, pushing the vision out of her head.

Tonight her husband had sunk to a new low, even for him.

Before the hole proved too expansive to dig out of, she told herself she needed to act—now.

Was that a shadow lurking in the distance? Was it Devon, arriving early, or had Augustus found her?

Her heart leapt with fear. No, nobody was there. It must have been the wind or possibly her mind playing tricks, for once she focused her gaze on the spot, she could see nothing but the trees close behind her.

Adelia purposely slowed her breathing. She would need to put her plan in place quickly, but for that, she would need to speak with Devon. He should be here any minute.

But, there was the sound again. This time, she was sure she heard footsteps, and when she called out, nobody responded. Now she stood, hands clenched in tight fists, determined to face the unidentifiable figure approaching from beyond.

There was nowhere to go, of course. No choice but to face the unknown. Adelia turned her head, her vision lit by the full moon above. She judged the distance from the edge of the cliff. There was no place else to go but down.

CHAPTER ONE
2017

THE CONSTANT MOAN of the foghorn in the distance soothed her. Hope never grew tired of her unusual home and its magnificent surroundings. Humming softly to herself, Hope dusted the small knickknacks that lined the wooden shelves. She stood back, hands resting on her hips, and studied the small lobby of the inside of the lighthouse.

Although the salty air remained chilled, the beginning of summer was just within reach, bringing flocks of visitors with it. Hope prepared for the first weekend of the season that the lighthouse would be open for tours.

Sighing softly, Hope wrestled with her contrasting emotions. During the summer, Amity Island bustled with noise, color, and activity. But with that abundance of energy, Hope often felt nostalgic for the quiet peacefulness of the off-season. Yes, life could prove to be a bit lonely here during those quiet months, but it was at those times she felt the strongest connection with nature and the island that sustained her.

For now, Hope looked forward to performing the job she did best: sharing her vast knowledge of the Amity Lighthouse and the surrounding Mayberry Bluffs. Soon, she would be conversing with bright, smiling faces.

Her mother would have worried, Hope knew, that she spent too much time alone. For most, a job was just that, an occupation. For her, this lighthouse was her life. It wasn't that she was a loner or a hermit. She was neither. At least, that's what she told herself. Hope did long for more interaction at times, but with the population of locals averaging around 1,000 during the slow seasons and many local businesses closing their doors for months at a time, she often experienced an aching loneliness.

"We're ready. Just like I told you yesterday and the day before that," Tracy commented. Hope knew part of the appeal of her job was getting to work so closely with Tracy.

"Yes, I know, I know." Hope twirled the ends of her wavy hair. "I just want everything to be–"

"Perfect." The two women spoke in unison.

Tracy closed in and grasped Hope's hands. "You worry too much. Everyone will love our treasured spot here. How could they not?"

Hope smiled. Of course they would. She glanced around at the old world, rustic charm. What wasn't to like?

"Of course, I'm just being silly." She clasped her palms around her friend's hands.

Tracy seemed to shift uncomfortably. Hope tilted her head, studying one of the few people she could call friend. She was lucky enough to share not only work with Tracy, but her house also. She and Tracy both resided in the small ranch style home on the property, situated about three hundred feet from the lighthouse. The ranch had been added to the property many years after the lighthouse was erected, in the year nineteen eighty-five.

"Is something wrong?"

Tears threatened to spill from the rims of Tracy's eyes. "I don't know how to say this, but . . . oh, I'll just come out with it."

Now Tracy had Hope's attention. "What is it?"

Reflections of light danced around her, tiny prisms of rainbows. "Oh my God!" Hope leapt a foot in the air. "You're getting married!" How she could have missed the gleaming ring was beyond her. It was tiny, yet clear, and, well . . . perfect.

"Yes, yes I am." Now the tears flowed freely from Tracy. Hope pried herself from her friend's grasp and stood back. Tracy sobbed openly, her breathing heavier. If this was happy news, then why was Tracy so sad?

"But I don't understand. This is wonderful news. Why are you crying?"

"Tommy wants to move to New Jersey. His uncle offered him a job at his company. It's a great opportunity for us, Hope."

Suddenly it all clicked. "No." Her hands dropped to her sides. She blinked back her own tears. This couldn't be happening. Hope didn't give her heart easily, whether it be to a friend or to a man. She couldn't imagine not seeing Tracy each day at work, at the home they shared.

"Please. Please say you're happy for me." Tracy's bright-blue eyes pleaded with her, misting over.

"I . . ." What an idiot she was. How could she take this news and twist it around to make herself the focus of this moment? Later, she would deal with her tangled emotions. She slipped her hand into her front pocket, feeling for the smooth stone she had found years ago with her mother on the beach. Hope considered it a reminder of her mother and it also served to soothe her; therefore, she was never without it.

She was, honestly, extremely happy for Tracy. She deserved every bit of this happiness.

"Of course I'm happy for you, Trace." Hope grabbed her friend and squeezed. She would be happy even if it killed her. "Does this mean—"

"Hope, you will find someone to help pay the rent at the house. The lighthouse foundation will let you stay on until you do."

Even if that were true, it wouldn't be the same, not without Tracy. "I guess."

"Let's celebrate." They locked up the lighthouse and headed next door to Tracy's car parked in front of their house. Tracy grabbed hold of her hand and Hope resisted, placing her feet firmly on the ground.

"What kind of celebration is this?" Tracy pulled back, a grin playing on her face as the wind whipped hair across her face. "Let's get out of here. You spend too much time here alone as it is. Come on, I know just the place."

It was true, the part about Hope spending too much time alone at the house. Although both women resided there, Tracy was a bit of a free spirit, and more nights than not, she was either with Tommy or gallivanting around the island.

Hope's stomach tightened as she reached into her pocket. It would be useless to attempt to change Tracy's mind about going out. Sucking in a deep breath, Hope swallowed then followed her friend down the driveway.

Hope didn't own a car and she preferred it that way. In fact, she had never even gotten her driver's license. Honestly, what was the purpose when living on such a small island? And walking was such great exercise, nobody could argue that point. The only time she regretted her decision was when it poured outside or when the snow blanketed the ground.

Tracy pulled out of the dirt lot and made a right toward the center of town as Hope's heart sped up a notch.

"Where to?" Hope peered out the window of the car.

"How about a burger and a beer?"

Morgan's had the best burgers in town with the perfect touch of small town feel. "Morgan's?"

"You bet." Tracy offered up a perky smile, then leaned over and rubbed her leg for a moment before she gazed out the window at a couple riding a bicycle built for two. "You know, I always thought that was the cheesiest idea." She pointed at the couple who shared the bicycle. "I mean, why not just ride your own?"

"I hear you." Hope had to agree with her friend's assessment. Who had thought to build such a strange thing? But she knew that this conversation was designed to distract Hope from her own thoughts.

"But that's just it. It's all about togetherness, you know?"

"I guess." But Hope didn't really know a thing about what it meant to truly be part of a couple. Why bother? Her life was here, on the island, taking care of the lighthouse. Most men would balk at the idea of joining her indefinitely on the island, and well, that was fine. Hope had decided long, long ago that she would never leave. Call it stubborn, call it whatever, but it was a fact. Hope considered herself responsible for Amity Lighthouse.

"One day, you'll meet someone so amazing you'll know

exactly what I mean."

But Hope didn't miss the way her friend's eyes turned away from her. Tracy knew her too well. It would take a very special person to dedicate his life to living on the grounds of the lighthouse, among other things.

Morgan's came into view and not a moment too soon. Tracy secured a prime parking spot right outside the tavern. In a few weeks, there would be a slim chance in hell that she could find such a spot; the tourists would be out in full vacation mode, snagging all of the best parking spots.

Several people passed them as they walked to the door of the tavern and Tracy earned a grin or a nod from each one. Practically every local on the island seemed to know Tracy and, as much as Hope had tried to deny it, she felt envious of Tracy's ability to converse with acquaintances so effortlessly.

Seconds after entering the pub, John, the owner of the pub, pushed himself off of his barstool and grabbed Tracy in a huge embrace. He barely seemed to notice Hope, and once again she felt that all too familiar stab in her chest. Who could blame John for not taking the time to make small talk with her? She knew it was her own fault since she didn't get out much, and therefore she didn't know him as well as Tracy, so she merely nodded and allowed John to usher them to a wooden table by the front windows. People watchers couldn't complain for lack of entertainment here. Hope took in the people riding by on their bikes and scooters, as well as the growing mid-day crowd walking by with an ice cream or package in their hands.

From their booth in the pub, they had a clear view of the bar in the next room. Tracy gazed ahead, squinting her eyes at something.

She followed Tracy's gaze and felt herself still. Placing

her hand over her chest, Hope gathered herself. She couldn't blame Tracy for staring, for she felt a small tug from deep within.

"Who is *that*? I haven't seen him around before."

Neither had Hope. She would have remembered this guy. It wasn't so much his handsomeness that struck her—heck, who was she kidding? This guy had an aura about him she couldn't deny; hell, she couldn't pry her eyes from him. This wasn't like Hope–not at all. She couldn't recall when she had last even noticed a man's looks or felt the magnetic force of attraction.

"I see you're just as spellbound as I am. Glad to see you're a living, breathing woman." Tracy winked at Hope, her blue eyes twinkling.

"I just—okay, fine. He's sexy as hell." She laughed despite herself. It felt good to be here in a different environment. Seconds later, that all too familiar feeling thumped at her chest. With sweaty palms, Hope motioned for the waiter, but he walked right by, intent on delivering food to the next table.

She needed something to drink. Fiddling deep in her pocket for the white stone, she ran her thumb across the stone's surface.

"You okay?"

"Yes. I'm fine."

Tracy caught the waiter's eye and requested two glasses of water, which he quickly placed with a thud before them.

It never failed. Whenever she strayed from the lighthouse, she had the sinking sensation that she was on borrowed time. She needed to get back. Fighting the wave that rose once more, she reached for the cold water.

"It's okay for you to leave. It's just a place, you know."

Tracy's voice dropped as she scanned the nearby tables. They had been through this before. Many times. Tracy called it agoraphobia. But Hope knew better. The lighthouse beckoned her, almost as if it had a pulse.

How could she possibly explain that to anyone, even Tracy? No one could possibly understand. Better for Tracy to call it by her scientific name. She was caught in a spell of sorts; that's the only thing Hope could equate the feeling to, for once she was back, she always felt safer and more peaceful.

"Come on. Get your mind on something else, like that divinely handsome stranger slinging beers."

Tracy raised her glass, and Hope sipped at her water. The cool beverage took her mind from her worries, and she actually found herself relaxing. It wasn't as if she never left her property. She did, just not happily and not for long.

This time would be different. She glanced at her watch and promised to stay more than an hour. She knew that times like this with Tracy would be few and far between, what with her moving off the island soon.

"We'll marry here, on the beach. I want you to be my maid of honor."

"I would be honored." Immediately, Hope's thoughts wandered back to the lighthouse, but then she forced herself to stare at the stranger behind the bar.

Amazing.

Her pulse slowed to a delicious crawl as she sipped at her water. The man turned his head and took that moment to stare right back at her.

"Oh." Hope averted her eyes and steadied her shaking hands.

"Did you just get caught checking out the bartender?"

Tracy was incredulous. She craned her neck to glance at the man and then laughed aloud.

"Stop that," Hope hissed.

"Don't look now, but I think he's on his way over." Tracy couldn't contain her grin.

CHAPTER TWO

1876

"Don't leave me, sweetheart. Stay in bed just a little longer, would you?" Augustus breathed deeply into her neck. Despite the heat of his stale breath on her, she shivered, trying to stave off the chill. His touch weighed upon her, stifling and demanding. She wasn't in the mood for this, for she had dreamt the same dream again. The one she couldn't seem to shake. It terrified her to her core.

"Surely you would like to eat some breakfast before starting your day, no?" She went to rise out of the bed, intent on having some space from him and a break from her own thoughts.

He grabbed hold of her chin, forcing her to face the quick flash of fury she spied in his gaze. "Why are you in such a hurry to leave? What else do you have to do today, besides take care of me?"

She shrank back, hating these outbursts, which she noted

were unfortunately occurring more and more frequently. She pried his hands from her face. "Let go of me, Augustus." Her firm tone matched his. He stared blankly at her.

"I'm sorry." He spun his head to face the small window. "I don't know what came over me."

And that was how it started, flashes of temper tamped down with apologies. Adelia hoped this was a passing phase. Her husband only needed to adjust to this new life of both beauty and isolation. The cliffs commanded sheer respect with their splendor alone. The bluffs also demanded fear. Many shipwrecks had taken place right here in her own backyard. The need for a lighthouse and a proper keeper was clear. This island hadn't been nicknamed "The Blundering Bluffs" for no reason.

With allure came peril.

But Adelia could manage to accept the whole package in order to make this her home. What proved to be more challenging was the change she witnessed in Augustus.

After she excused herself from the bedroom, Adelia padded her way down a small flight of stairs to the simple but charming kitchen and busied herself with the task of preparing a fortifying meal for Augustus and herself. Soon, she would have clothes to wash and her usual daily chores of tidying up their home. Beyond that, Adelia would have to admit that she, herself, felt the faint touch of boredom beginning to affect her.

Regardless of the weather conditions, each day Adelia walked through the fields and edged her way to the bluffs. Today, she would do it again.

What Adelia longed for was a friend. A soul to whom she could speak, confide her worries to, spend time with. She had yet to find such a person here on the island. On their rare walks or rides by horse into town, Augustus would always conduct his business of buying necessities with small talk, but that was all he did. Seemed he mastered the art of meeting acquaintances, keeping true friendship at arm's length. A few times when they had first arrived on the island, Adelia made the walk into town herself and had stirred up casual conversation with several of the local ladies. She had been quite pleased with the adventure and had hoped to make a habit of walking into town at least a few times a week, weather permitting, and after her housework was completed, of course.

Lately, though, Augustus discouraged her from wandering into the village on her own, even forbidding her to take the horse, which Augustus borrowed from time to time when he needed to gather large quantities of goods from the village. Claiming that some minor burglaries had taken place in town, he deemed it unsafe for her to make the trip on her own. Augustus strongly felt that he held the power of the final say on decisions of both his life and hers. But to make matters even worse, Augustus expressed concern over her short walks to the bluffs as well. This time, she wouldn't budge—there was no way she would give up her time on those cliffs; the solitude and scenery served to soothe her soul. It seemed the only release to keep her centered. She figured what Augustus didn't know wouldn't harm him, and it was such a short walk. Not once did Adelia feel nervous or apprehensive.

"Smells wonderful, darling."

Adelia stiffened as strong hands captured the small of her back. His obtrusive words had startled her. "Thank you."

"Will you be joining me this morning?"

"Of course."

Why did he ask these strange questions each day? She sat down to eat the first meal of the day with him each time she cooked. She always had, and prior to them arriving here at Amity Lighthouse, he had never inquired. Yet another oddity of his behavior.

"I apologize for my rudeness earlier. I do know that, like me, you have many important tasks to attend to each day. I don't know what came over me." He sighed, burying his face in her shoulder from behind.

Adelia clamped her jaw tightly as she closed her eyes. It was the pressure getting to him, that's all. She loved this man, and she would stay by his side, help him through this transition in their lives. A new home and a new job would be enough to cause stress to anyone. Besides, at times like this, she could see clearly the man she had fallen in love with.

She shook her head, and she spun to face Augustus. It would all work out.

Pressing her body against his, Adelia smoothed his hair and kissed him on the mouth.

"Now that's better, darling. Watch out or you will burn our food." He pointed to the rising smoke from the small stove.

"Oh my goodness. You've gone and distracted me, Augustus." She pressed down on her skirt and cleared her throat.

"Later, I will show you what it means to be properly distracted, Adelia. For now, let's eat." He winked at her. Yes, this was the Augustus she knew—clever, witty, and charming.

Adelia handed Augustus the warm bread she had buttered for him and sat back for a moment to take in their new home. Augustus winked at her as he munched on the bread. They would be fine here. She swore at times her mind worked in overdrive, picking apart details and looking for trouble. Releasing the tension from her shoulders, she grabbed her juice and took a sip.

"What are you up to today?"

"Oh. The usual chores."

"And after?" He peered at her from behind his glass of water.

"I haven't given it much thought," she lied through her teeth. The bluffs beckoned her, and she didn't wish to hear his opinion on the dangers of walking the area alone.

"Well, I certainly hope you don't wander off the property, my dear."

Her heart sank with each word he spoke.

"They haven't caught the troublesome man yet, you know. And from what I hear, people are being cautious. Staying close to home, you know?"

A flicker of emotion she couldn't name crossed his face, and then it vanished. For the first time, she considered that Augustus could very well be making up this tale to keep her from making friends. Would he go as far as to mention it to others, though? She had witnessed the conversation between her husband and one of the men in town. Straining her mind to recall the details, she kept her focus on Augustus.

Yes, he had to have been the one to bring up the subject in town that day; of that she was certain. And if Adelia remembered correctly, she thought the other man had seemed oblivious to the news, as if hearing it for the first time.

"Who told you about this man?"

There it was again. The distant look in his eyes as her old Augustus slipped away. "Who?"

"Yes, Augustus. Who?"

Rising from his chair, he left his plate for Adelia to clean. "I don't recall, and what kind of question is that anyway? Do I question every word you speak?" His voice grew louder with increasing agitation. She watched as Augustus stood and faced the window overlooking the vast ocean. He turned, as if to speak to her, but then shook his head and stormed off.

Just as she had thought, he didn't have an answer. Adelia's shoulders tightened as she sat, watching her husband disappear into the darkness of the hallway.

CHAPTER THREE
2017

"Everything okay here?"

Not wasting any time, Hope gulped back a sip of the beer the bartender had just placed before her. She figured that would shut her up, before she said something utterly ridiculous, as she always did when faced with awkward social situations such as this.

"Yes, we're great. Thank you so much for asking." Tracy spoke clearly and offered up a wicked smile, along with a firm handshake. "I'm Tracy, and this is Hope. She apparently lost her voice." Hope made a mental note to strangle Tracy once she got her alone.

"Hi," Hope squeaked, accepting the man's hand as he introduced himself as Clooney. Despite herself, Hope's pulse sped up, and she felt a tug at her chest.

"Now that is an unusual but lovely name," Tracy gushed, her eyes darting back and forth between Hope and Clooney.

Hope had to admit the name was an attention grabber, just like the man himself.

Clooney glanced back and forth between the two women before his gaze settled on Hope. "Do you live here year-round?"

"She does." It seemed Tracy couldn't help herself.

"I do, and I can answer for myself." Hope's eyes bore into Tracy.

"Ah, so she does speak." Clooney chuckled.

Heat spread across her face and chest. One of the curses of being fair: her flushing gave away all of her emotions.

"I'm sorry, I didn't mean to embarrass you." Clooney stood back, but his eyes remained on Hope.

"Oh, it happens to her all the time." Tracy laughed aloud.

"Thanks, Trace." Hope reached for the stone in her pocket as she took a breath. "No worries, Clooney."

There. Now she slowly felt her confidence growing. She could speak to a man on her own without interference from Tracy. Her friend would soon vanish off the island, and Hope would have to try to find other friends. The very thought was enough to make her cry if she let herself. Instead, she focused her attention on the handsome bartender.

"Good. Listen, there's a pretty decent local band playing here later tonight. I figured I'd stick around and hang for a bit after work if you ladies feel like stopping by."

Her first instinct was to blurt out an excuse as to why she couldn't make it back later, but then she hesitated and touched her smooth talisman. "We'll be here."

"I . . . uh." Tracy whipped her head in Hope's direction, shocked into silence.

A giggle erupted from Hope, and damn, she had to admit it felt good, *really* good. Getting out of the house later and enjoying herself was an entirely different matter, but she would concern herself with that when the time came.

Could she do something as simple as enjoying a band with a cold beer? She wanted to, but then she thought of a hundred reasons why it would be a bad idea. She caught the eye of a couple seated next to them at the bar and winced.

Why did people choose to stare at her like this? It was hard enough feeling shy in social situations, but so often, so very often, she noticed the stares from strangers pointed in her direction. She was exhausted, so tired of feeling like a strange alien intruder wherever she went. What she needed to do was work harder at trying to fit in. She managed one last look at the couple beside her, who were now hunched over, whispering to one another.

"We'll be here." She repeated the simple phrase that held the power to possibly change her circumstances. Her mother's face came to mind, and Hope knew if her mother was around, she wouldn't be pleased with the fact that despite her friendship with Tracy, Hope had turned herself into a near recluse.

Thinking about coming back here later to meet up with Clooney scared the crap out of her, but there was an undeniable quality that Clooney exuded, plain and simple. From the messy wave to his hair to the way his shirt lay half out of the jeans that molded his body, he was all man. But the best thing was that Hope didn't pick up any vibes that Clooney was a player. Although he approached her and Tracy here, she had a gut feeling they were an exception.

"I guess we'll be here, like the lady said." Tracy gave Hope's thigh a quick tap under the table and beamed.

Clooney dismissed himself, getting back to his work behind the bar. "I'll see you tonight." He waved at them both, but his gaze lingered on Hope.

"Well, well. What do you know? There might just be hope for you after all, Hope." Tracy winked. "No pun intended."

All Hope could do was laugh.

THE BREEZINESS THAT had come over Hope just hours earlier eluded her. Now that she was back in the arms of her beloved lighthouse, she cursed herself for having second thoughts. Damn Clooney and his rugged, handsome looks.

Damn, damn, damn.

No outfit seemed right for sitting at a pub, listening to a band. Her mind wandered back to the couple at the bar—staring, whispering . . .

Warning bells rang out as clear and persistent as the foghorn in the distance. That settled it.

Where the heck was Tracy? After searching their small home, she figured Tracy must be at Tommy's place. Picking up the phone by the kitchen table, Hope walked to her front door and stepped outside. The beckoning lighthouse stood before her, grand and majestic.

How could such a building evoke both comfort and fear? She pondered the question as she waited for Tracy to pick up her cell. Ring after endless ring brought forth images—speedy visions of the recurring dream from the night before.

In her dream, she walked the dark lighthouse, up, up, up the swirling narrow staircase, spying only her bare feet below. It was always the same. In the dream, she stopped on the floor of the lighthouse that housed the old bedroom that was no longer used, but rather was restored to appear as it had in the late 1800s when the building was first erected and then lived in.

When the tourists arrived each season, she would stop here and walk around, proud to walk with Tracy and show off the living quarters, from the bedroom to the small kitchen and bathroom. But lately these rooms gave her pause, for she dreamt of them more and more.

Who was the figure that slept soundly in her dreams in that bedroom? Try as she might, Hope never actually saw the face of the still form under the covers. Then, her visions would continue as she passed the other rooms in the grand building. If she listened carefully enough while in the dream state, Hope could hear her own shallow breathing. With it, her heart sped up, slowly at first but then faster and faster until the sound seemed to echo off the walls; as if the house itself had a heartbeat. She and the house became one, sharing vehement emotions.

Ultimately, it always ended the same, and this was the part of the dream that seemed to increasingly dominate her mind: she would arrive at the tippy top of the endless spiral steps, and she would see only the bare feet below her own body. There would be the endless pause where she would suck in her breath, her heart racing wildly until she heard the voice. She would wait a brief second, hoping it wouldn't come, but it would. A male voice. Calling out, over and over. Each time she willed herself to breathe deeply in order to attempt to stop the claustrophobia pressing her body, sucking the life from her.

Then came the worst part. She never saw his face; how could she even attempt to overpower a faceless man? But the outcome never differed. Oh, how she wished it would, for it felt so terrifying and so real.

When the push finally came—like the hands of a clock moving forward, the shove would arrive—her body descended.

Down.

Down.

Down.

Like a rag doll with no power to change its fate. As if she were boneless, she bounced down those dark, hopeless stairs. The only sound echoing in her ears was her body hitting the steps and her own scream, until seconds before she hit the bottom.

Right before that damning moment, she would wake, covered in sweat.

"Hope. Hope!"

Hope freed herself from the thick trance, now recalling she had her phone in hand, Tracy on the other end. "Tracy. Sorry, I'm here."

"Geez, you got me worried there for a moment. You okay?"

With shaking hands, Hope assured her friend she was fine. She gripped the railing on her porch and took a deep breath. "Yes. Listen, I'm not feeling well, but why don't you and Tommy go ahead to listen to the band tonight?"

"Oh no you don't! Hope, I haven't seen you like you were down at that pub, well—ever. I'm not going without you."

Hope gazed from the luring lighthouse to the mysterious ocean beyond. "Then I suppose you won't be going either. I bet Tommy would love to go; you should reconsider."

"First of all, Tommy is heading off on the first ferry of the morning tomorrow. He has a meeting with the company, and no, this is unacceptable."

Of course, it was. "Please, Tracy. I'm just not up for this.

Respect my feelings here."

The brief pause allowed Hope to still her shaking hands. Maybe it would do her some good to escape for a few hours. That nightmare continued to burn in her mind, increasing her anxious thoughts ten-fold.

"I don't mean to sound cruel here, but what will become of you when Tommy and I leave the island for good? I need to know you'll be fine on your own."

"I'm always fine on my own."

"You're alone quite often, I'd have to agree with that, but the fine part? No. You need to do this. I have a feeling about that Clooney guy, and I know you feel the same."

Hope knew the guilt Tracy felt each time she left the house to spend time with Tommy. Her friend shouldn't have to feel ashamed to get on with her own life.

Clooney's brown eyes came to mind. His kind smile floated through her thoughts, lightening the recent tension. It was true, there was something about Clooney—she couldn't deny it. But still.

"Come *on*. You can do this. Didn't we have fun earlier? It would be the same— only better. This time, we'd be hanging out with Clooney, listening to the band . . ."

For a moment, Hope allowed herself to imagine what could transpire this evening. She pictured herself sitting there, Clooney on one side of her while Tracy sat on the other. It would be as if she were carefree, just one of the local women letting loose and blowing off some steam.

But she wasn't the typical woman, and she never would be. The wind picked up, hitching her breath slightly. Hope's hair whipped in the increasing breeze, and the ocean churned just a shade darker, or so it appeared. Just like that, her dismal mood returned.

"I can't." Her voice croaked out, barely a whisper as she stroked the stone in her pocket over and over.

Silence on Tracy's end ensured that her friend knew she had made up her mind. "I'm sorry, Tracy."

"I'll be home soon. You can still change your mind."

But she wouldn't waver. Hope knew she would settle in with one of her books and maybe a glass of wine. It would be the same as last night and the night before that.

CHAPTER FOUR

1875

THE WEDDING NIGHT

ADELIA GAZED INTO her husband's dark eyes. She couldn't believe it was true. She was actually married to this remarkable man. As of a few hours ago, as a matter of fact.

Their courtship had been brief, but she knew a keeper when she met one. Augustus was kind, wise, and full of passion for her and for life. She loved the way he spouted off fact after fact on any given topic. He was so intelligent about the world around him, and she couldn't deny how safe he made her feel.

She couldn't wait to start this next chapter of her life as his bride. Spinning the ring on her left hand, she could hardly pry her eyes from the sparkling diamond and simple gold band.

"What are you thinking?" Augustus pulled a piece of her hair loose from the tight bun she wore.

"Just that I'm the happiest I've ever been."

"Why is that, beautiful?" His eyes rested on her lips as he placed a gentle finger over them.

"Why do you think, silly?" She batted her lashes at him.

"Oh, maybe because you're my wife?" he teased, eyes alight. "That's a pretty impressive thing."

"Well, maybe you're so happy because you had the privilege of marrying me!"

"Shh, I think we're both happy because we found one another." Augustus silenced her next words with a deep, lingering kiss.

If this was what her new life would be like, she never wished it to end. If she could just lie here with Augustus by her side, holding him forever, then she would be content and never wish for anything more.

"What now?" She wiggled her brows playfully, her pulse quickening delightfully. She had dreamed of what would come next since she had laid eyes upon him.

"We travel to Amity Island and make our dreams come true."

His statement was unexpected; she had been speaking of their first night together as husband and wife. What was this talk about Amity Island? "What do you mean?"

"I didn't wish to spring this on you before, but I got a job. A really good job." He reached for her hand and held it steady, smoothing her palm gently with his long fingers, over and over.

"I–I don't know how to respond to this news." She shook her head to clear her thoughts. Amity Island? Why, that was hours away, and in order to reach the island, you would have to travel by steamboat.

"Tell me that you're happy. Tell me I did the right thing by accepting this job."

She didn't wish to appear ungrateful, but the news hit her hard. "Augustus, I'll be away from my family and friends. My mother . . . "

"I know you and your mother are close, but we can have her as our guest, and everyone else for that matter, as often as you'd like. Imagine this: living on the beautiful, majestic island and having much more living space than either of us are accustomed to now."

He spoke the truth. Here, Augustus had a menial job, and both of them had still been living at home with their respective parents. The plan was for Augustus to get a better job, and then they would find a small living space to call home. She loved Augustus with all her heart, but he wasn't particularly well off financially, and neither was she. They were spending their wedding night on the top floor of his parents' house.

"Spacious living, the roar of the magnificent ocean? Island living? What could be better than that, especially together, arm and arm? Imagine the children we would raise, running through the field we will call our backyard." He continued to finger her palm, making small circles. "Tell me you're ready for our grand adventure. Tell me you're ready to trust me." He was so wise; it was one of the things she loved best about him.

His eyes held so much hope. How could she possibly deny him this dream he had crafted for the two of them? Knowing how hard Augustus had worked to set up this life for them, she felt touched. She was a romantic at heart, and now she was finding that Augustus matched her so well.

After all, what could be more romantic than leaving everything behind and starting a brave new adventure together, as husband and wife?

She trusted him.

"I'll do it."

"Yes!" He smacked his large hands together and grinned widely. "Now, what was that you were saying before?" He winked at her.

"Get over here." She pulled Augustus close, then closer still, until they were as one.

CHAPTER FIVE
2017

She should have gone. In her heart, Hope knew it to be true. She was her own worst enemy at times, couldn't seem to get out of her own way. That did it. Any chances of hitting it off with Clooney were surely ruined; he would think that she had no interest in him.

Glancing at the clock on her kitchen wall, Hope sighed. It was approaching nine o'clock, and the band must have been in full swing. She had watched Tracy leave to venture out alone, assuring her friend she would be fine on her own at the house.

A glass of red wine usually succeeded in helping to ease some tension. Hope made her way to the cabinet by the fridge and peeked in. Yep, there was still a bottle left. She slowly uncorked the wine, her mind still on the pub back in town. After pouring the wine, Hope grabbed a sweater and headed for her lawn chair outside, near the edge of the property. The view never ceased to stun her. This is what she lived for, this tiny piece of happiness and peace up here on the cliff.

Slowly and deliberately, Hope sipped at her wine, savoring the pleasant hints of cherry and chocolate. The sound of gravel crunching in the distance caught her interest before a faint light came into view from behind her house. Who could that possibly be at this hour?

Standing up, Hope clutched her wineglass, pulling it against her chest. For the hundredth time, she wondered if she should have some kind of weapon to protect herself up here, at this desolate home—especially at times when Tracy went out, which was happening more and more.

And soon you'll be all alone, all the time.

She fought the dark emotions threatening to take over. Headlights shone over the property, bringing her back to fearing solely for her physical safety. Tracy wouldn't be home so soon. For now, a quick prayer would suffice in keeping her safe.

That, and the token in her pocket.

"Who's there?" She rose, squinting through the darkness.

Who was that, whispering and giggling like school children?

"I said, who's there?" Now her chest thumped at the continued laughter. But wait—that laugh was all too familiar. "Tracy!"

Tracy came through the shadows with Clooney by her side. Both smiled as if they were in cahoots with one another, which they quite obviously were.

"What are you guys doing?" She could scarcely believe her eyes. Later, when she had Tracy alone, she would give her a piece of her mind.

But then, she noticed the apprehension in Clooney's gaze, and she figured it couldn't have been easy for him to be cajoled into doing this. Tracy was downright relentless when she wanted to be.

Clooney offered her a sheepish grin as he held up a bottle. "Tracy told me you like red wine, and the band wasn't that great after all, so Tracy talked me into stopping by."

Tracy's eyes pleaded for forgiveness. Hope knew she had only been trying to help, but honestly, sometimes Tracy just needed to mind her own business and respect Hope's wishes.

Alas, Hope caved. "Fine. Come on; I was just enjoying a glass of my own by the cliff. I'll grab a blanket and open that wine."

"We'll be right here." Tracy grinned as she spread her arms wide.

Although taken by surprise, Hope had to admit she was excited to see Clooney. Her heart flip-flopped whenever his gaze bore into her. She could hardly contain her grin as she grabbed the blanket, two more glasses, and the bottle opener. She was on her own territory here, and that could only make it easier for her to relax and enjoy the evening.

The blanket was large enough for all three of them to sit comfortably. Hope poured the wine into each of their glasses and settled back to enjoy the roar of the ocean in the darkening distance.

"This is beautiful, but it must get lonely for the two of you. What do you guys do to occupy yourselves up here?"

Hope felt as if the question was directed more at her since Tracy was the outgoing one who had ventured to the bar alone. Either that, or it was her sensitivity about the amount of solitude her life contained.

Clooney's inquiry was the million-dollar question. He

had asked the question that most hadn't dared to, but she could see the curiosity in the expressions of others, and had been waiting to respond the only way she knew how.

"I enjoy the beauty of this island around me and consider myself lucky to be a part of it. But remember, Tracy and I have each other and plenty of company once the visitors arrive, which will be soon. Very soon."

Clooney raised his glass to his mouth. She watched him sip the liquid and licked the dryness from her mouth.

"Ah, yes. But then, what about during the winter months? I imagine it could get a bit lonely up here."

She watched him take another sip of his wine. He watched her from behind the rim of his glass. Now what could he be thinking of to evoke such a look?

Clearing her throat, Hope took a gulp of her wine. He had this affect on her that she could honestly admit no other man had. And she barely knew him.

"Well, at times, I suppose. But overall, I wouldn't change at thing. This here—the lighthouse and the bluffs—this is my home." She glanced at Tracy in the darkness. "Our home." It was as if she felt the need to protect her surroundings. Tracy remained uncharacteristically quiet.

"I envy you both. I do." He glanced around the property, his eyes fixed on the top of the lighthouse.

His words caught her by surprise. Most people scoffed at the thought of living at this isolated spot. "You do?"

"I do. If I were you, I'd stay here, well, forever." Clooney glanced down, staring into his glass. His words seemed solely meant for Hope.

A chill coursed through her body, inch by inch. She shivered as she pulled her sweater closer to her body. The image of the winding stairs from her dreams pushed forward in her mind. Those bare feet, the darkness . . .

"Was it something I said?" Clooney's intense stare rendered Hope speechless.

"Nope, that's just how she looks now and then," Tracy offered, finally breaking her silence.

"Please, give it a rest, Tracy." Hope then directed her comment to Clooney. "I'm fine."

"I hope I'm not intruding here."

"No, no. I'm glad you came. Really." Hope had enjoyed this visit so far and had to admit she was glad Tracy had been so bold as to bring Clooney back with her.

"Then I'm glad too. And I'm going to get going soon, I have to be up early. It was wonderful seeing you both."

Hope glanced at the additional car in the driveway. "I'll walk you to your car," she stated as she stood to join Clooney.

"It was great seeing you again, Tracy. Don't be a stranger down at the pub, you hear?"

Tracy saluted with a grin. "Oh, you'll see me around. Have a good night, Clooney."

Once they were at Clooney's car, he leaned back and studied Hope. Neither spoke as the air filled with a feeling Hope couldn't deny. Anticipation and attraction sparked around them as Clooney moved forward. He brushed a stray hair from Hope's face and then returned his hands to his sides.

"I was disappointed when I didn't see you at Morgan's tonight."

"I'm sorry, I—"

"No, don't apologize. When Tracy asked me to join her here, I wanted to come but also worried that I was stepping on your toes. I hope you don't think I'm pushy."

"No, I don't."

"You just seem . . . different, somehow. You stand out from the rest of the women I've met. I had to take the chance and try to get to know you."

She gulped, unable to respond.

"There's something about you I can't quite put my finger on. Something—mysterious."

It was as if he could read her mind, for she thought the same about him. Almost as if she had known him a while, or known him before. But that was ridiculous, of course.

Then he leaned closer, and his voice took on a husky note. "I want you to know that I want to kiss you, right here, right now."

She swallowed hard, not taking her eyes from his intense stare. This moment, she knew, she would recall for a very long time to come. She held her breath, helpless to do anything but wait for the feel of his mouth on hers.

"But I won't. Not tonight."

Her body responded as her heart sank. It took all of her strength not to call out for Clooney to go ahead and kiss her. Hell, she felt like pulling him in and tasting his wine-stained mouth right now.

"But trust me. I will."

Her chest thumped wildly as she nodded at his simple yet profound words.

"And when I do, you won't soon forget it." He touched her hands briefly as she felt an undeniable spark, then he turned to get in his car.

Hope watched his car disappear down the driveway, clutching her hands over her chest.

CHAPTER SIX

1876

"Just one moment, please." Adelia turned toward the sound of rapping at the door. It wasn't often that she and Augustus received visitors up here on the bluffs, and with her husband's recent decline in behavior, she looked forward to a distraction. Brushing her hands across her apron, she smiled as she approached the front door.

The man who stood before her appeared to be around her age, maybe slightly older but not by much. "Hello there. Can I help you?"

"Sure hope so, miss." He turned his head to point behind him. She followed his gaze and listened to him explain how he had gotten lost on his walk through town.

"Well, sir." She cleared her throat and chuckled. "I hate to tell you this, but you're far from town—a couple of miles— and it's getting pretty dark." She pointed upward. The fading sky overhead seemed to be darkening by the moment.

"Shoot, then. I traveled far off the beaten path." He grinned, showing off his attractive face.

"Ah, yes. Listen, my husband is just upstairs working. Let me see if there's anything we can do for you. Wait right here, okay? Oh, what was your name again?"

"Forgive me for being rude. I didn't say, but it's Devon."

"Devon. I'm Adelia MacGregor." She nodded her head and studied him for a moment.

"Adelia. What an interesting name. I like it."

"Thank you." Adelia was surprised to feel heat rising to her face as she scurried back inside, leaving Devon on the front step.

"Augustus?" She took the endless, winding stairs as quickly as she could manage. Gasping for air, she wondered when these stairs would prove easier to manage. Shouldn't it be getting easier? They had been here several months and the stairs still challenged her on a daily basis.

Why wasn't he answering?

"Augustus?" she managed, though out of breath. She had almost reached the top of the lighthouse now. "Augustus."

There he stood, eyes straight ahead on an unknown point, transfixed.

"Augustus?" Her voice croaked out, barely a whisper. "Augustus?"

The setting sun streaked across his face, displaying shadows which played on his blank stare. Almost afraid to touch him, Adelia placed a finger mere inches from him, ready to reach out.

But then, he snapped to attention, startling Adelia. "What is it? Can't you see I'm working up here?"

Actually, no, she couldn't. But of course she wouldn't dare utter the words. More and more lately, she stumbled upon

Augustus doing nothing but staring straight ahead into the distance. Quite honestly, this bizarre behavior rattled her. If she knew how to approach the topic, she would have, but for now, she remained silent.

"I–I'm sorry. Listen, someone is downstairs, at the door. It seems he is new to this area and got lost. I'm concerned, just sending him off in the night."

It hit Adelia that Augustus might very well worry that this was the notorious robber in town. She waited him out, hoping he wouldn't embarrass her by causing a scene with the man downstairs. Adelia felt the pull for a friend, some sort of company once more.

"Well, well." Her husband's face lit up. "Why didn't you say something earlier? Company, you say?"

She couldn't predict his moods at all anymore. Relief coursed through her, and she relaxed her shoulders.

Apparently, Augustus brightened at the thought of another person up here at the lighthouse besides her. Hell, Adelia felt the same. How pathetic was it that the highlight of their day, week, was a lost neighbor?

"Come on, we can't just leave the poor man standing out there, can we?" Adelia bit her lip. She never quite knew what to expect with the mood swings Augustus displayed lately; he was up, down, and everything in between. But for now, he was up, and she would take it.

Augustus reached over the sill for his glass of gin and took a swift swig. It seemed that glass was present more often than it wasn't as of late.

She followed his frantic steps downward and watched as Augustus opened the door, practically pulling Devon indoors. He pumped his hand, then ushered Devon inside their kitchen to the table.

"Sit, sit. You must be exhausted," Augustus exclaimed.

"Actually, I'm fine. Just a bit lost." Devon's eyes found Adelia across the room. "Your wife was kind enough to open the door to me."

"Yes, she is very kind. Adelia, darling?"

Augustus had taken to calling her darling more frequently, and she had to admit the tone he used while speaking the supposed endearment unnerved her.

"Yes?"

"Do we have enough food to offer the man some dinner? He must be famished. What is your name, sir?" Augustus rambled on.

"Devon." Adelia managed to blurt out his name before Devon had the chance. This earned a glance from Augustus.

"Devon Bane here." Devon broke the silence.

"Devon," Augustus stated deliberately. "I'm Augustus, and obviously, you already know this is Adelia." There was an audible pause. "Would you like to stay for dinner?"

"I wouldn't want to put anyone out." His glance bounced from Adelia to Augustus.

"That's nonsense. What kind of neighbor would I be if I didn't offer to feed you after a long walk?"

Adelia wrung her hands together. She fretted that she did not have enough stew to serve another person.

"Adelia, darling, we do have enough to include Devon here, don't we?" Augustus raised his brows. He set his jaw out, waiting for her response.

"Of course, yes." She would simply do without her share of the meat. Dinner for her tonight would be the vegetables, gravy, and bread. The option was far better than listening to Augustus complain endlessly after Devon left for the evening.

He would lecture her about making more food with each meal so that they could eat the leftovers for lunch the following day. Usually she accommodated him, but earlier, when Adelia had noticed they were in need of some items from the store, she sought Augustus out and found him once more with that faraway glaze in his eyes and glass in hand.

"Then it's settled. I'm going to finish up a few last minute tasks upstairs, and then I'll wash up. Say thirty minutes or so, before dinner?"

"Sure." Adelia held her breath until Augustus disappeared from view.

"I hope I'm not putting you out. I don't have to stay, you know."

She waved her hand in the air. "Devon, don't be ridiculous. We'd love the company." But she hurried to the stove and stirred the pot as she directed Devon to make himself comfortable.

"Would you care for something to drink? We have water, milk, gin."

"Milk would be wonderful. Thank you, Adelia."

Adelia grabbed the container of milk from the icebox and poured a glass for the two of them. No doubt, gin would be the beverage of choice for Augustus when he returned. Another subject she felt unsure of how to approach. Clearly, Augustus was drinking too much, and it seemed he was starting earlier and earlier with each passing day.

Unsure of when the shift in Augustus, their marriage, had begun, Adelia frowned. When had she started fearing her husband's moods? She couldn't recall the specific moment; it was more of a gradual shift, she supposed. The bigger question was whether she could ever get back to enjoying her husband's company instead of fearing it. A new thought struck her as she wondered if it was the isolation of being on the island or something else. Did this behavior run in his family? Was he only now showing her his true colors? She realized that she knew next to nothing about his family history in terms of medical conditions.

"Well. Isn't this nice?" He was back, and much earlier than she had anticipated. Augustus glanced down at the two glasses placed on the table. The flash of irritation from him could have been easily missed if she didn't know him as well as she did. Adelia watched for a reaction from Devon, but he sipped at his milk, oblivious to the snapshot of what her life was slowly morphing into.

"I was going to ask you what you'd like to drink. I figured you'd want more gin, though, seeing that that glass of yours is never far from your side." It slipped out; she hadn't intended to say the words, but for now, it felt good, and she would deal with the repercussions later.

The remark wasn't lost on Augustus, for his dark stare promised the conversation would, without a doubt, continue later.

This time, Adelia knew Devon felt the unease in the air. He cleared his throat and took a gulp of his milk, careful to keep his eyes to himself.

In a swift movement, Augustus reached into the cabinet and pulled out a glass. With a loud thud, Augustus lay his empty glass on the counter, his penetrating gaze causing Adelia to flinch. "I'll have milk. Just like the both of you."

For weeks, the only beverage Augustus had chosen to drink with his dinner was that damn gin, but she, too, could make believe all was well in this house atop the cliff.

Any outsider would have claimed that the dinner went well, that conversation flowed freely and laughter warmed the room.

Only Adelia and Augustus knew differently—and Adelia worried what kind of game she and her husband had started and just how far this treacherous path would lead.

CHAPTER SEVEN

2017

W<small>HILE</small> T<small>RACY</small> <small>FLUTTERED</small> about the kitchen, making wedding plans, Hope took every ounce of strength she possessed to make the trip down to Morgan's Pub to see Clooney. She supposed it was only fair; he had, after all, summoned up his own bit of courage to join Tracy at her house the other night.

Heading outside, she mentally prepared herself for the walk into town.

She could do this.

She would do this.

Alone.

By this time next week, her cherished lighthouse would be full of sunburned vacationers, wishing to hear about the history of the building and grounds.

Legend had it that a woman haunted her very lighthouse. At first, Hope had scoffed at the ridiculousness of the tale.

She figured no fascinating vacation destination was complete without a frightening ghost story or two for people to sink their teeth into. Supposedly, this woman was killed at the hands of a man, most likely her husband, and therefore, she made it her purpose to haunt men for all eternity. Ha! Well that might explain why she herself had never encountered the ghostly spirit. The entire story had held no merit in Hope's opinion. If there was anything amiss, she, of all people, would have sensed it.

But then came a thought: what if?

A flash of bare feet on the lighthouse steps blinded Hope. She felt faint and paused to catch her breath for a moment.

Just a dream.

Only a nightmare.

Subconsciously, she had probably conjured up the fearful thoughts based on that ghost story. But those recurring images stole her breath away every time she experienced the vision. When had the nighttime drama intensified? There was no doubt in Hope's mind that the dreams were happening more and more lately; now, almost on a nightly basis.

And then, she pinpointed the timeline. Sure, Hope had experienced the nightmares many times, but since meeting Clooney, it was definitely getting worse. She knew the reason for this: it was anxiety, plain and simple.

Soothing her soul, she remained standing in the driveway, her hands running over the stone in her pocket until she could draw a full breath. She would not allow anxiety to mess with her relationship with Clooney. Oh, no. Hell no. It was time to get herself together and grow the heck up.

With new determination, Hope breathed in the soothing smell of the beach and ocean in the air and made her way down the road leading into town. The whipping wind slapped at her face, but it refreshed her and gave her the energy she needed for surprising Clooney.

As suspected, the town had grown even more crowded today, as summer was around the corner. That's when it hit her.

Hard this time.

Sweat pooled over her entire body as she felt a vise-like clamp over her chest.

Breathe. Breathe. Breathe.

Hope lifted her quaking hands and swallowed back her nausea. Closing her eyes, she placed a hand in her pocket and took deep breaths, in and out.

In and out.

Hands went instantly to her pocket, searching for her calm center.

In and out.

"Dammit!" Hope's chin trembled as she fought back tears. She moved to the side of the road and sank down to the ground, clutching her knees to her chest as she waited for her quiet hell to pass.

What she would give to be able to get through her day, performing tasks with low stress that most people took for granted. "What did I ever do to deserve this?" She spoke aloud to herself as she fought back rising tears.

She had no idea how long she had been sitting there, but eventually, the haziness that had consumed her slowly cleared, allowing her to focus her thoughts and breathe with ease.

She needed just a moment longer, to still her shaking thighs and compose herself before she made a total fool of herself. Even the stone failed to calm Hope this time.

Heck, if she fell apart this early in the game, how would

she manage to even say hello to Clooney? Minutes ticked by as Hope felt the pull.

Go home.

Just go back to the lighthouse and you'll breathe again.

The lighthouse . . . lighthouse . . . lighthouse . . .

This was not normal.

Far from it.

She knew it, but knowing something and being able to change it was an entirely different matter.

There, on the street, she had the all too familiar internal battle until finally Hope gathered her courage and stood. She had this. What really got her moving was recalling that amazing feeling of happiness she experienced whenever Clooney was near. She trudged the miles into town, praying the cold chill of her own sweat would continue to dissipate.

"Hi there." Hope tried her best to appear friendly as she passed a woman she had seen several times in town. Although the woman didn't reciprocate Hope's greeting, Hope wouldn't allow her thoughts to travel down the usual dark path. Maybe the woman hadn't heard her. Yes, that could be it, Hope told herself, biting back the sting of rejection. It was okay; the woman just didn't know her very well. At least Hope had tried, she had made an attempt to fit in.

With a refreshed attitude, she forced a smile, stuck her hand in her pocket, and headed straight for Clooney.

His back faced her as he reached into the cooler behind the bar. She watched him then turn and tidy up a small spill before he turned in her direction.

Their eyes met and held. For a brief second, neither moved nor spoke. Clooney's eyes glazed over as his mouth fell slightly. She wondered if she had been wrong to come here.

Then he smiled and headed straight for her. "Well, well, well. I can't believe my eyes." He winked, lightening the mood. "To what do I owe the pleasure?"

She smiled widely, hands splayed out on the bar in front of her.

"Oh, I was in the area and wanted to pop in to say hello."

"Hello."

"Hello." She couldn't contain her grin.

"So is that all? You said hello. Now what?" He smirked, and his mood was contagious. She didn't mind the teasing, it actually helped to relax her.

"Now—now I sit, and *you* can grab me a beer."

He studied her, leaning forward on his elbow. "Really? The lady shows her bossy side. I kind of like it." He winked once more.

"That's right. And I'm only getting started." She returned the wink, feeling lighter than she had in years. Who was this girl? She barely recognized herself but didn't stop. She continued to ride the wave because it felt so good.

"And I'm only getting started with you. You'd better watch yourself, Hope, or you won't be able to get rid of me if you keep it up."

"Ha! What exactly do you intend to do with me?"

That sobered him up. Suddenly, the moment took on a serious tone. "Sweetheart, you have no idea what I wish I could do with you right now."

"Oh."

Clooney had succeeded in silencing her with his words while making her heart pound furiously.

He leaned over and placed the slightest kiss on her forehead. It could have been mistaken for a friendly gesture by an outsider, but to Hope, it was so much more—just a touch, a mere brush, but enough to cause her senses to reel. The kiss earned a stare from the man sitting near the end of the bar. What was his problem? Hadn't he ever seen a man kiss a woman hello before? She steeled herself to ignore the glare from the stranger and focused instead on Clooney.

"Hey, Clooney, what the hell are you doing?" John called out, eyeing him from across the bar.

"Sorry, boss." Clooney shrugged his shoulders and grinned. "Ah, yes. I need to get back to work. What do you think of me coming to pick you up later, maybe take you to a movie? I hear the theater is pretty cool."

The unique theater still maintained its old world charm. Hope knew the history of the building well as she had enjoyed herself the few times she had visited. It was built in the late 1800s and first served as an amusement area before transitioning to a theater house. Hope hadn't been to a movie in years, and as much as she longed for some semblance of normalcy with Clooney, it would be too much for today.

As if he sensed her hesitation, Clooney squeezed her hands tightly. "Tell you what. How about I bring—wait, hold on a minute." Hope watched as Clooney's eyes sparkled with mischief. He pulled a bottle of red wine from under the shelf. "How about I stop by after work and bring this?"

It was the same brand of red he had brought to her house a few nights earlier. Between the bottle and his sweet grin, she was smitten. How could she say no to him?

"I would like that very much."

"Then let me get back to work, and I'll see you, say around 7:30? I'd like to go home and shower before heading up to your place."

"Then get to work, Clooney," she teased.

Clooney leaned in once more and whispered into her

ear, causing a trail of goose bumps to linger delightfully up and down her body. "I like the way my name sounds coming from your mouth." He traced small circles over and over on the inside of her hand. It soothed her, almost as if she were holding her precious stone. She closed her eyes, imprinting this moment in her mind.

He was going to drive her crazy right here in the middle of the pub if he wasn't careful.

She turned to leave and nearly smacked right into Tracy, who stood directly behind her, Tommy by her side.

"Hi guys!" Hope offered cheerily. She couldn't figure out if Tracy was happy to see her or upset. Her stare lingered.

"Trace? You okay?" Hope narrowed her eyes.

Tracy's eyes darted toward Clooney, who was occupied serving drinks. "Yeah, sure."

"I'll see you guys later; I'm heading home now." Hope leaned in and whispered to Tracy, "I have to get ready. I'm having company later."

Tracy's jaw fell. Hope didn't wait for her friend to respond before heading outside, feeling light and breezy.

CHAPTER EIGHT
1876

For better or worse, she had found her friend. The only problem was that Augustus would never understand or accept Devon as her ally, because one, Devon was a man, and two, Augustus considered Devon to be his own confidant.

There was nothing going on with Adelia and Devon romantically. Adelia wouldn't allow herself to consider it, although in the dark of night, she had to admit that her mind had wandered down that forbidden path once or twice—only in her mind, she told herself, where she kept her desires to herself and nobody, including Augustus or Devon, could truly see.

Adelia noted moments when Devon would stare at her just a moment too long. It didn't take a genius to imagine Devon might have similar thoughts. She only hoped Augustus hadn't caught those stolen glances between them. She wouldn't act on it, not even in the slightest. She wasn't like those unfaithful women whom she had heard of and had judged harshly. Then, what was going on in her mind? The old Adelia would have never even entertained such thoughts.

My God, was she, too, going mad just like her husband? Was she heading down toward a spiraling madness? She mentally erased her traitorous thoughts.

She and Augustus hadn't shared in any acts of physical intimacy in months, not even the slightest kiss. What happened to the man who had wanted a large family, who had claimed the more children they raised, the merrier?

Up until now, Adelia had refused to admit to herself how truly troubled they were and how much damage had already been done to their marriage. If she swept their hardships under the rug, they ceased to exist; that had been her saving grace as of late.

Adelia didn't wish to admit defeat. Over and over, she told herself this difficult time would pass, and she prayed she would have her old Augustus back. Until then, her lonely soul was fueled by the companionship she had found in Devon.

Neither she nor Devon had planned or expected to hit it off so well, but it just seemed to happen. The first few times she had seen Devon after that night he had knocked upon their door, they had shared polite, if distant, conversation. Most of the time, she had brought the men coffee in the sitting room, then left them to take care of her chores.

It was the one time when Devon had come calling and Augustus had walked into town that triggered their deepening friendship. After that, she felt more comfortable with each visit. He was, after all, their only company at the lighthouse.

One thing they hadn't yet dared to discuss was the

feelings they may harbor for one another, or, for that matter, the deterioration of Augustus.

Instead, they chatted about life on the island, how the isolation had made them both lonely. They had each shared how their new relationship helped to ease the restlessness, which plagued them both.

Augustus hardly showed his face most days until dinnertime. Sometimes he would request that lunch be brought up to the tower, and sometimes he stated that he wasn't hungry.

God only knew what he was up to. She had lost her taste for going upstairs the past few weeks to see what he was doing while he worked, only climbing the steep stairs occasionally, when need be. She couldn't stomach the sight of Augustus, his eyes glued to the damn window, that ever present glass of gin no longer on the ledge of the tower, but rather in his hand, ready to sip at a moment's notice.

One of these days and soon, she would be forced to bring up the subject of his drinking—and the staring, which went on for hours, or so it seemed.

Which had come first? Drowning himself in gin or staring endlessly at nothing? She wasn't sure it mattered.

"Adelia! What the hell is the matter with you?" His harsh statement broke her train of thought. She pushed her hands into the pocket of her apron and spun to face her husband's wild, accusing stare.

"I don't understand." Her head shook in time with her hands. She must have been so deep in thought she hadn't heard him calling.

"Do you think I enjoy having to walk up and down sixty-five narrow steps to get your attention?"

Had he seriously counted the steps? She made a mental

note to find out exactly how many steps actually led up to the top.

He had a problem.

They had a problem.

Enough was enough.

To hell with playing the pretending game. She intended to discuss her best course of action with Devon today, when he came by for their daily walk, which would be in a few minutes.

"I'm sorry, I didn't hear you." She flushed, watching Augustus tighten his jaw as a thin sheen of sweat formed on his upper lip.

"Yes, you must have been so wrapped up in your *chores* you didn't take note of me hollering out your name, over and over."

"What is it you wanted, Augustus?"

"Devon is due to arrive any moment now. I asked him to come over, and I expect that you will have something to offer my friend to eat and drink, my darling."

Sarcasm dripped from the endearment as it more frequently did. *His* friend. Of course she wasn't permitted to share a friend of his. Back before they had arrived at the island, they had shared plenty of friends.

"Yes, of course." That would mean Devon would be late for their walk. But what could she say?

"Augustus?" She waited for him to respond but then continued when he didn't answer. He simply peered at her from behind his glass of gin. "Remember when we first arrived and you promised I could invite my family and friends for a visit?"

He swung back another sip of his poison. "I never promised that, you're out of your mind." He drew closer, his long fingers pressing down on his glass. "Do you really think anyone wants to come visit right now? It's dark, cold, and dangerous."

Dangerous?

Goose bumps raced over her body.

Well, it could certainly be chilly as it was autumn, but not horribly so and, of course, the sky darkened each night, but *dangerous?*

"It's not dangerous." She scoffed out her response and quickly realized her mistake.

Like a tiger stalking its prey, Augustus pounced, pulling her forward by the collar of her blouse. "Stop! You're hurting me." Her breath came in spurts as she rose a shaking hand to attempt to push him off her.

"*I'm* hurting you? *I'm* hurting you?" he repeated, spittle spraying from his mouth, hitting her face. She closed her eyes, forcing him out of her vision. "What do you think will happen if this *criminal* wandering town approaches you or someone from your family?"

The *criminal?* Although she was almost certain this burglar was fictionalized by Augustus, the possibility this man could indeed exist gave her pause.

"We would pick up my family in town, in broad daylight, Augustus. What could possibly happen?" Her mother's face came to mind. Oh, what she would give to see her mother's face, hear her sweet, calming voice.

"Nobody comes and nobody goes." He swiped his hand through the air with finality, slurring his words.

"But Augustus—"

"You're lonely?" He faced her, a naked madness in his eyes. "Get a cat. It'll help keep the damn mice under control."

Adelia clutched her palm over her chest, her heart aching

for the life she had envisioned for them; she would even take the life she had on her own before Augustus, but not this.

She watched Augustus stumble on one of the narrow steps as he ascended up, up, up, to the place where he spent more and more time. One of these days, if he wasn't careful, he might just tumble down those stairs for good. Gin didn't mix well with the life of a lighthouse keeper.

The image of him falling took over her mind as she fought to vanquish it. What had just gotten hold of her? Adelia shook from the fear of her own thoughts. Was it fear for him that shook her so, or was it wishful thinking? What frightened her even more was that the image was so close, so very similar to the recurring nightmare she failed to eradicate from her mind.

Adelia walked over to the icebox and pulled out a few items for Augustus and Devon. She needed to get out of here fast before she experienced any more frightening thoughts. Augustus would just have to serve his own guest. Why not? Lately, she found herself scolded and in trouble for nothing. Why not give him something real to be angered by?

She grabbed a light jacket from her bedroom closet and headed downstairs for the door. Knowing she wouldn't have as much time with Devon today as she normally did, she sighed, but at least she could steal a few moments away with a sane, breathing person.

What if Augustus turned his gaze from the sea to the field one day when she wandered off? What would Augustus do if he found out their little secret? She wondered if he would even care but somehow knew that he would, if only for purposes of control. Lately, he spoke of what proper wives did, cooked, and how they behaved. Heck, one of these days, she would enlighten him on the bizarre ways in which *he* conducted himself.

Was *he* showing the behavior of a proper husband? Adelia chuckled bitterly as she thought of the gin-swigging fool her husband had become.

His list of complaints were endless: she wasn't giving her chores full effort, she shouldn't have missed the speck of dust, should have cooked the meat a minute longer. Adelia could do nothing right, or so it seemed. At times, she bickered with him, even gave it back to him. Once she had complained that he could lift a finger to help if he wasn't happy with the way she kept the house. That comment wouldn't be spoken again.

And the craziness went on. His latest kick included boasting about the lighthouse and their attached home. "I built this house on blood, sweat, and tears." He repeated this over and over the other day. Adelia corrected him, stating that he did indeed make a living from the house, but that another man had actually built it. Several men had joined together in constructing the lighthouse, including the iron work. Augustus certainly did not participate in the building stages.

Did her husband actually believe the nonsense he spouted so venomously? Regardless of his lies, she knew Augustus wasn't even the first keeper. The original keeper of the lighthouse had started a year earlier than she and Augustus had arrived.

Now the lighthouse was their responsibility, and with that obligation, there came a price. Had the previous, original keeper experienced a similar cruel fate? A thought intruded her mind as she ambled her way to the door. Soon she would make a trip into town to see if the doctor would speak with her. How did a normal, loving man change so drastically in a matter of months? She shuddered, taking in the stifling brick walls closing in on her. She tried to catch a full breath, feeling as if Augustus and this place were suffocating her.

Glancing carefully over her shoulder, Adelia closed the door, then exhaled once she knew she was safe to leave this fortress she called home.

NORMALLY, DEVON WOULD be sitting, waiting at the bluffs. She bounded out of the wooded area and approached the top of the desolate cliff alone. It won't be long, Adelia thought, scanning the steep, adjacent cliffs and the rocky beach below.

Many people would be scared half out of their wits, standing atop the commanding cliffs, no proper fencing in sight. Not Adelia; this place brought her peace, even before she and Devon had made it their meeting spot. She stood, as minutes passed, her mind circling around the madness of her marriage.

"Adelia," Devon called out from behind.

Something was wrong. She heard it before she could turn and read trouble in the lines of his face. Weariness and fatigue showed through, despite his meager attempt at a smile.

"Devon." She was by his side in an instant. "What is it?"

"Hush. It's nothing to for you to worry about." But his stature said otherwise. Devon ran a swift hand through his brown hair, avoiding eye contact.

"If it involves you, it most certainly does." She hadn't meant to blurt out the admission. With burning cheeks, she bit her lip and spun her head to gaze out at the rough whitecaps in the ocean below. Each time she and Devon met, she felt that inevitable pull increase, forcing her to meet her own betraying thoughts head-on. Her feelings tangled around and around, clouding her judgement. She was getting too close. She would not, *would not* cross the dangerous line from which there was no coming back.

"Adelia." He stated her name gently, pulling her toward him. The sound of her name coming from a gentle, kind man such as Devon only served to remind her of the monster her husband had become. Her name spilled from his mouth once more, softer this time. Visions of her and Augustus on their wedding day, then their trip to the island grabbed hold of her. Before she could even enjoy the fond memories, something darker, then much darker, invaded her soul.

No. No. No.

Now all she could see was that damn gin, his spittle, the way he stumbled up and down those menacing stairs.

Harsh sobs wracked her body; she broke at the feel of his touch.

"Adelia. Look at me." His firm tone commanded her attention. He soothed her with his touch, his words.

If just his touch alone provoked so much emotion, what would happen if she faced him, gazed into his soulful eyes?

He took charge, giving her no choice but to look directly at him. He gripped her shoulders, shaking her harshly.

She didn't trust the storm taking place in his eyes. Didn't trust her own heart.

Adelia cried openly as Devon then pulled her close and stroked her back, over and over, until her cries were silenced and she could catch her breath. The moment had passed— for now.

But what about next time? She had been seconds away

from touching his full lips with her own. Moments away from disaster.

"Listen to what I'm going to say to you, Adelia, and listen good. I think we both feel this . . . " Devon's wavy hair whipped in the wind, and at that moment, she felt as if he was the most handsome, soulful man she had ever laid eyes on. Her heart betrayed her mind as it grabbed hold of every word he spoke.

Afraid of what might tumble out of her mouth, all she could muster was a nod of her head. This was it—this moment held the power to change her fate. If she acted on it, her soul would never be the same. If she didn't, she might regret the chance to find her happiness in the enveloping darkness.

"I can't—I won't do this." Biting her lip, she turned her glance away from Devon, toward the rising ocean below.

Gently now, Devon placed his hands on her arms. "I will not take another man's wife. I won't do it, not even to an enemy, let alone my friend. As troubled as Augustus is, I suppose he is still a friend, although it's getting harder and harder to call him that each day."

She knew he must be looking for the same thing she searched for—the traces of the old Augustus that shone through in rare, fleeting moments. He paused, as if choosing his next words carefully.

"What I'm going to tell you might be difficult to hear, but damn, I'm going to say it anyway."

She swallowed the lump that had formed in her throat. Gazing up at him, she waited him out, trying to silence her thumping chest.

He reached out and tenderly wiped a tear from her cheek. Leaning in, he kissed the other side of her face. She tasted the saltiness of her own tears. He then lifted his hand to move a strand of hair behind her ear. Suddenly, his expression darkened and his eyes grew serious. "You need to leave him."

"What? I can't—"

"He's not well. He doesn't treat you right. He doesn't deserve you."

She shook herself free from him. He didn't understand, couldn't comprehend her situation. "It's not about what he or I deserve, Devon. Don't you see? I made a vow, a promise to stand by him. I thought you said he was your friend. What kind of friend tries to coerce a man's wife to leave?"

"I know what I said, but it's not black and white here. I'm afraid he's gone mad. He spoke of you today. It's why I was so late. Hear me when I tell you, Augustus is not right in the head. It's not safe, I worry he could cause serious harm to you if you stay."

The flash of a vision blinded her but only momentarily. "Devon? I have to tell you about the dream."

"What are you talking about? What dream?"

She lifted her eyes and shared each horrifying detail of the nightmare that stole her breath, and she confessed it was occurring more frequently with each passing day.

She left him speechless, saw the worry etched on his face. "Devon?"

"I–I don't like this. It's just a dream, but, Adelia, you need to do something, before it's too late. Talk to him, tell him you're not happy here, isolated on the bluffs. Blame it on the loneliness, but tell him, tell him you need to go back to your family."

She had thought it before, and the words played again in her mind. *You're a big girl—a woman now.*

"He is my family." She sobbed at the soberness of those

words.

Devon winced and turned to pace the grass below their feet. He tore a hand through his hair and then stopped to face her. "Is this about stubborn pride? Some marriages just aren't meant to be. He wasn't what you thought when you married him." Gingerly, Devon pulled her head toward him and held her close, so close, pressing the tip of his nose to hers, maintaining eye contact.

"Would you have married him then if he behaved the way he does now?"

She tried to free herself from his grasp. Damn. He already knew the answer, but Devon wanted to hear the words from her lips.

"Answer me, damn you." His voice rose in agitation. He knew the answer. Why did he insist upon hearing it?

"No–no, I wouldn't have. But I don't take my vows lightly. I promised to marry him in sickness and in health. The Augustus I met is there. Deep inside, I feel it. I think I just have to get him off this island, away from the lighthouse. If we go back home, I know he'll recuperate."

"Recuperate? My God, Adelia. This isn't typhoid fever!"

"No, you're right, Devon, it's not. But what ails Augustus is a sickness. It's a disease of the mind."

"Hell, Adelia." Devon released her and stepped a few feet away. "He won't get better, he won't. You need to go—alone."

Picturing herself leaving, having that conversation with Augustus, caused her such duress she couldn't see past it. "He'll get better. I'm going to talk to the doctor soon. There's got to be something he can do. It can't be hopeless."

"I can see that I'm not getting through to you. I fear you will find out in your own time, in your own way. And I do hope you're right, Adelia, I do. I would wish nothing more than for you to be happy, even if it means he gets better and you stay with him." Devon's voice hitched on his last words.

She turned to peer out at the threatening sky and the tumultuous water below. "I will stay with him." Adelia held her head high, fighting back more tears.

"It's a mistake." His deliberate words reached her heart because she knew, for now, it was his last attempt to change her mind.

"It's *my* mistake."

"Yes. Yes, it is."

She had hurt him. From the hunch of his shoulders, she knew he worried not only because he harbored feelings for her, but he also fretted for Adelia's safety.

"But Devon?" She dared to look up at him.

He nodded, waiting for Adelia to continue. Quick fear replaced the stubbornness she had displayed only moments before.

A sort of twisted desperation enveloped her. "What am I going to do about him?" She grabbed Devon's jacket, pulling him in. "What am I going to do?"

His answer came in actions, not words, as he drew her in close. So close, she felt as if nothing in the world could touch her, harm her. This is what she had hoped to find in Augustus—the feeling of being kept safe from harm, protected from the harshness and cruelties of the world.

She could have stayed there in his embrace all evening, but then she remembered that Devon was about to tell her something. What was it that Devon had mentioned about Augustus? "What did he say to you today?"

"He said that you were acting strangely—quiet, different. He worries that you're not in the right frame of mind to wander off the property by yourself."

Pulling back, Adelia nearly stumbled on a rock behind her. So he was aware that she walked off the property.

"What?" That's not what Augustus had said to her. Augustus spoke of the dangerous man who wandered the town, but this?

"Just what I said. He wants to keep you prisoner with him, up on the cliffs in his lighthouse."

"*His* lighthouse?" A chill seeped through her veins. "Is that what he said?"

"I'm afraid I speak the truth. He confided in me that although not many are aware of it, he was not only one of the builders of the lighthouse, but the one and only keeper."

"No, I—no." Adelia paced the top of the cliff, walking, spinning, from one end to the other, her surroundings closing in on her, making it difficult to catch her breath. She gazed down at the churning water below, feeling fear drop to the pit of her stomach.

"I told you, he's gone mad." Devon closed in on her, gripping her arms firmly.

He didn't have to tell her what she already knew to be true.

CHAPTER NINE
2017

"WHEN AM I going to get to take you on a real date?"

She scrunched her nose. "A *real* date?" But she knew what he meant. He wished to take her out: dinner, the movies . . . normal stuff. If she didn't get her act together soon, Clooney might lose interest. Each time they had seen each other from the first time they had met weeks ago, he had come up to Hope's house to hang out with her.

"Can we just enjoy tonight?" On the outside Hope smiled, but inwardly, she cringed. How long could she go on with this charade?

Suddenly, a thought hit Hope, filling her with optimism, but then her enthusiasm crashed, leaving her with the broken pieces of reality. How would Clooney react if she did tell him the truth? The lingering possibility was right within her reach, so close she could practically touch it.

"What is it?" Clooney placed his wine glass down on the

table, his eyes scrutinizing her face.

Should she or shouldn't she? After deliberating the thought a bit more carefully, Hope made a decision. For better or worse, it felt right.

"Come on, I want to show you something." She reached for his hand, feeling a jolt at his touch. She pulled Clooney forward and hurried her pace, heading outdoors and toward the gothic-style brick lighthouse. The moon lit their way to the building across the field as Clooney huffed from behind Hope.

"Whoa, easy there."

"What's the matter? Are you out of shape or something?" she chided him, and damn, it felt good to lighten up. He had that affect on her. Hope smiled to herself, thinking that she just might be addicted to the idea of Clooney and the feelings he released from within her. If only he accepted what she was about to tell him, that is. Her mood bottomed out as she worried about the outcome of the secret she was about to unleash.

"What's gotten into you?"

Hope knew it was easy for her to fall back and question whether this was the right move. She needed to act quickly before she changed her mind. If Clooney couldn't handle the truth about her—*all* of her—then she supposed they weren't meant to be. But she sensed he would understand; it just felt right when they were together, and he was so different from most of the people she had known in her life.

Releasing his hand, Hope unlocked the front door to the lighthouse. "Come on." She turned to see Clooney gazing around the ground floor of the building she was so proud to call home. Hope flicked the light on, illuminating the bottom of the spiral staircase.

"Where are we going?"

"Come, you'll see." She walked hand in hand, with him huffing and puffing while she made the trip with ease. Neither spoke as they continued up, up to where the staircase narrowed to the very top of the lighthouse.

It was here, at this focal point of the structure, where she felt her strongest emotions. Maybe it was because Clooney stood by her side, but tonight the feeling was stronger than ever. Fear and uncertainty, her unwelcome visitors, soon overpowered traces of comfort and peace. The vision of those bare feet, *her* bare feet, she assumed, slammed into her, hard and fast.

Clooney gripped her hands, pulling her close. "What's the matter?"

She didn't respond at first, just relished the rush of happiness she felt in his embrace. Just as soon as the frightening moment had arrived, it dissipated. There. Now she could gather herself together; now she could breathe.

"It's—it's nothing." From the peak of the sixty-eight-foot octagonal, pyramidal tower, she peered at the dark sky and even darker ocean thrashing below. Hope noticed the way the light of the sapphire-blue lens played on Clooney's features. She took a few deep breaths before attempting to speak. This was her moment to clear the air, to lighten her burden. This was also the moment that could destroy their blooming relationship and stomp it to pieces.

She swallowed and prayed she was doing the right thing. "Look at this, all of this. " Hope's whisper grew louder. She slowly spread her arms wide, showing the expanse of the outdoors just beyond her tower.

Your prison.

No. The phrase taunted her, echoing inside her head.

Your prison.

"No!" She held her head, attempting to wipe out the words.

"Hope. Are you okay?"

Judging from his confusion, Hope knew she had no choice but to tell him everything.

She tamped down her emotions and picked up from her thoughts before the uninvited intrusion. Reaching for the stone in her pocket, she rubbed the smooth surface before facing him.

"What do you see when you look outside?" Hope's voice softened, growing serious.

"What do I *see*?"

"Yes. How does all of this make you feel?" She gestured toward the blackness of the rocky cliffs.

Scrunching his brows, he turned and faced her.

"No, look. *Really* look." Gently, she took hold of his chin and directed him toward the tower window.

"I think—I think it's absolutely amazing. The beauty of the sky, the moon, the ocean, you . . ."

"Be serious." Her eyes pleaded with him.

"Okay. Like I said, it's all breathtaking. I would imagine it's even more picturesque during the day. All this darkness takes away from it."

Yes. Yes, it did. The darkness seemed to have a way of provoking her uneasiness even more.

"Why do you ask? What's up with you?" Clooney pushed a stray hair from her eyes.

She could do this. She *could*.

Clooney, of course, would see the beauty of the outdoors and beyond. Maybe it was his ability to see the good that attracted her to him.

"When I asked you what you saw, how you felt, you answered the question like most would."

"I don't understand. "

"The view, outside, everything—" Her pulse pounded in her ears; the blood rushed through, making it difficult to continue her train of thought. This was a mistake. He wouldn't understand. Only someone who experienced the wash of fear that was always spread thickly over the beauty of the world would get it.

"Breathe. Just breathe." He pulled her close, holding her there without the need for words. Right now she only needed to calm her racing heart. He seemed to understand, and for that she was grateful, as they stood for minutes, pressed together.

Courage eventually replaced the uneasiness and she knew it was time. "I don't see the world the same as you." She paused, but then decided to spit it out—all of it, before he had a chance to break her momentum. "Instead of awe and beauty, I feel fear. In place of happiness and a sense of contentment, I see a crippling impossibility." She brushed away the moisture rimming from her eyes as she finally released her breath and allowed him a moment to process her admission.

Clooney's mouth hung open, his eyes searching hers. Then he did something terrifying: he stepped back. Back against the railing of the tower, away from her. This was ludicrous, she should have waited. My God, what had she been thinking? Way too early. It was *way* too early in their relationship to share her darkest secrets. Now she would pay the price for her misstep.

"Clooney?" The desperate edge to her voice rang out in the tower. Her feelings swayed from disappointment to hopefulness, and then back again as she kept her feet grounded to the spot. She stared down and willed her feet to stay put before seeing bare feet instead of her own shoes.

It was there. Then it was gone.

The image had surfaced at the worst possible moment, but she didn't break. She washed the bare feet from her mind until all she could see were her own shoes once more.

Anxiety.

Just anxiety and fear.

She had proved she could be strong before. She could tangle through the sticky web again. She had, after all, been dealing with it for as long as she could remember. It hit Hope that she couldn't recall a specific timeframe when she wasn't weighed down by her fears and agoraphobia. And for that matter, she didn't seem to remember much of who she had been before this plague consumed her.

"You have agoraphobia." His eyes bore into hers.

His simple statement lifted her from her troubling thoughts, directed and commanded her attention back to him. "What?"

"You're afraid. My God, why didn't I see this before?" Slowly, Clooney ran his hands through his hair.

A single tear lingered on her cheek and then fell. She reached for him, but then she backed away before she could feel the sting of his rejection.

Clooney paced the floor, his footsteps pounding the intricate honeycomb pattern design that so many tourists had been enamored with. What would they say now if they saw the scene before them? No normal person could empathize with her. Her hand clamped down tightly on her stone.

Then Clooney stopped, rooted to the spot—and he

did the most amazing thing. She wouldn't forget, not if she lived to be a hundred years old. He opened his arms to her. Stepping into his embrace, she released her hand from her pocket. Hope's heart soared.

He got it. He understood.

At that moment, she knew in her heart that she loved this man. Gazing up at him, there was no question he felt the same. No words were necessary as he pulled her toward him, gently at first, but then took charge and grabbed hold of her head, pressing his mouth on hers with an urgency neither could deny. The jolt she had felt upon touching Clooney before dimmed in comparison.

With all senses on high alert, she kissed Clooney back with every fiber of her being. Thoughts of panic and agoraphobia were distant memories. Right now, her heart pushed out every part of her body, including her mind. It was Clooney, all Clooney.

"Hope?" He broke the kiss, and she wanted nothing more than to pull him back to her, but she also needed to hear what he had to say.

"What?" she managed, her breath coming quickly.

"This may sound crazy, but I think I'm falling for you."

He was falling in love with her.

He *understood* her.

And just like that, she was home.

CHAPTER TEN

1875

FIRST FERRY RIDE TO THE ISLAND

"Four or five, at least." Augustus smacked his lips down on hers, causing a stirring deep inside. Since their wedding night a few days back, Augustus inspired feelings from within Adelia she had never known existed before.

"Four or five? *Children?*" Adelia pulled herself from his embrace momentarily. "You're crazy, Augustus!" She swatted at his thigh.

"Crazy for you, my love." He grinned broadly, scanning his eyes on the impossibly blue ocean beyond their spot on the steamboat.

"Look, the sky and the ocean are almost the exact same color. I feel like we're living a dream." With one hand, Adelia pressed her ornate bonnet firmly on her head, and with the other, she pointed out at the expanse of the sea and sky.

"We are. And Adelia?" He turned her face to his. "Don't wake me up." Pressing his lips to hers, he smothered her with his exuberance and passion.

"Augustus, look, we're not alone." She giggled as she motioned toward the other passengers on the boat, who were doing a decent job of pretending not to notice their display.

"Fine, fine. But later, my wife, later." Augustus squeezed her palm as they gazed in silence at the breathtaking landscape.

Adelia's mind wandered from her husband and the new life he promised them to thoughts of her family and friends. She missed them already. Would they make this trip to the island to visit her? If so, how often would it even be possible? She was a woman now, a wife, in fact, and that meant Adelia would have to grow up and center her life on making her own family. Her eyes misted, and she turned her gaze away from Augustus, not wanting to upset him. He, too, had made sacrifices in order to give them a chance at a brand new life. She fidgeted and stuck her hands in her pockets to still them.

"What is it?" His thumb and pointer finger turned her chin toward him so that she was forced to look him squarely in the eye. "Aren't you happy?"

The dam broke, and her tears flowed freely. "Oh, husband." She sighed, considering her next words carefully. "Of course. I'm just feeling an abundance of emotions I suppose."

Her shoulders dropped when she saw his expression soften. "That is only natural, Adelia. I bet you feel excited, exhilarated, a bit frightened, and melancholy for those we left behind. Am I right?" He leaned forward, kissing the tip of her nose.

He was exactly right; he always was. "Yes, that's precisely how I'm feeling. Is that how you feel, too?"

"Yes. Don't you think I'm scared as well? But look at the big picture. We're in this together."

Together. Yes, he was right.

"Together, like a grand adventure." He cuddled her so close that she couldn't deny the feelings of warmth and security she felt as she leaned her back against her husband's chest. Here, she felt safe.

"They'll want to take our photograph once we arrive on the island. The town has a photograph of the first couple that watched over the land and wish to keep up the tradition." He kissed the top of her head. That sounded just fine to her.

She was almost in a state of complete relaxation until Augustus began fumbling for something in his pocket. "What are you doing?" She turned to see what he was up to. He removed a small bottle and took a swig.

"What is that?"

"Relax, my Adelia, it's just a bit of gin, is all, in celebration of our new lives." He took another small sip, and she settled back against him. "Just close your eyes and dream the sweetest dream, for that's what is to become of our lives together." He patted her arm, and she closed her eyes for a moment.

Adelia felt her body move in rhythm with the waves and gave in to the sense of peace that was slowly taking over her body. She watched as the steamboat drew closer to their destination. The cadence of the water below allowed her to release the tension and worry about leaving her old life behind. They would be fine—great, even. Her eyelids felt heavy, and she gave in, shutting out the sunlight.

His arms gripped her firmly, then tighter still, until she could scarcely catch her breath. "Augustus, you're hurting me!" He spun her around so that she faced him. He crushed her arms, madness gleaming in his eyes.

"Let go of me!" She tried to escape his clutches, but he was too strong. She could barely register his maniacal laughter before he tossed her forward. It was then she saw the stairs below her bare feet, tripping, stumbling down the endless spiral of dark stairs.

Descending to the depths of blackness.

She woke, startled, right before she hit the bottom. Moments before she faced certain demise.

"Adelia, Adelia!" Augustus shook her, clearing the last cobwebs of the dream from her mind. "You're dreaming, Adelia. It's okay; I have you." He rocked her, kissing the top of her head as she tried to make sense of what had just happened.

"You just had a dream, that's all."

Adelia sat upright as she spun her head to face him. "It–it wasn't a dream. It was a nightmare. A horrible, awful nightmare." She bit down on her lip, but then felt relief to see kindness in her husband's eyes, not the stark hatred she had just witnessed in her dream.

"I'm here. It was a dream, just a dream," Augustus repeated once more, hushing her until she lay against his chest. After a few fitful attempts to find slumber once more, she gave in and then faded into the oblivion of sleep.

CHAPTER ELEVEN

1876

"I NEED TO see if I can speak with the doctor. Maybe he can give me some insight as to how to deal with Augustus." She twisted her hands, forming a tight knot. Even to her own ears, she knew it was a lame answer to a compounding dilemma.

"And then? Then what? Is there medication that can help him?" Devon pried her fingers apart and forced her to look at him.

"I don't know. I'm still trying to imagine how he could have gone from my dream husband to my worst nightmare." Adelia flashed back to that memorable boat ride over to the island. Was that nightmare just a random stream of consciousness?

Or was it more?

A premonition of sorts?

It was no accident that Adelia no longer took the long

walk up those spiral stairs unless she really needed to speak with him. She had even stopped walking around barefoot most of the time. Instead, she sported thick socks. As if socks could stop him from going mad.

Adelia chuckled harshly, earning a glance from Devon. "What's funny?"

"Nothing. It's not even worth explaining."

"I'm wondering if Augustus is finally showing his true colors." Devon tapped his fingers on his thigh as they sat in the tall grass overlooking the bluffs. In the daylight, the bluffs appeared less threatening than they had last night, lit only by the moon and stars above.

She had wondered the very same thing but had since dismissed the thought. "No. That's not it. I only wish you could have met him before. He was a different man, so full of hope and life. It's as if the lighthouse has sucked the breath out of him."

"He shouldn't keep you so isolated up there. It's not healthy. You should have never listened to that nonsense about the thief in town. He's making it up to keep the both of you prisoners."

"You might be on to something there. What I can't figure out is why he allows you in our lives." She had pondered the question and came up with only one viable answer. Augustus selfishly wished for a friend—for himself. He had no idea he was sharing Devon with Adelia, and if he discovered their secret meetings, there would be hell to pay.

"He's bored, and you help him pass the time. Once upon at time, not so long ago, my husband was quite social. He's beginning to despise me and longs for some form of companionship, which I can no longer give him."

Nodding his head, Devon reached for her hands but

kept his gaze on the ocean below. Adelia directed her own gaze to the rough waters. She thought for a moment of the numerous shipwrecks that had occurred right here and then considered that with the help of Augustus manning the lighthouse beacon, all of the shipwrecks he must have prevented. At least he knew how to do his job. For as many times she had caught him staring blindly into space, the light always beamed brightly, the tower remained spotless, and a fresh coat of paint decorated the walls. When he found the time to complete such tasks was beyond her since most times she only saw him staring blindly out the window.

"You mean the world to me, Adelia. I won't let anything happen to you, not if I can help it." He squeezed her hands tighter.

The vow wasn't meant to be cryptic, but she heard the waning of Devon's voice as he spoke the latter part of his promise. As long as she stayed in the lighthouse with Augustus, she was at risk.

"I have to try. He's my husband." Adelia peered at the ground and refused to make eye contact, for she didn't want to see the hurt in his eyes.

"I know, Adelia. I know. I just wish—"

This part would be the most difficult part yet. If she were to remain focused on helping Augustus, it required that she did the job with her entire being. Even if that entailed losing Devon.

"Stop, Devon. Listen to what I'm about to tell you." She gathered her courage and mentally rehearsed each and every word she would speak. "I cherish you, Devon. I cherish this—us."

"You don't have to do this, Adelia. We've done nothing wrong." He had to know what she was going to say, and it killed her to turn him away, but it was the right thing to do. The only thing she had control of at this point.

"Let me finish. My time with you has been memorable. In so many ways, Devon." Her voice broke; this was proving to be more difficult than she had imagined. She took a moment to gaze at Devon, tears misting his eyes. She knew in her heart, she had been so wrong about Augustus, even from the very start. As kind and wonderful as her husband had once been, he wasn't the man she was destined to spend her life with. She knew Augustus was a lesson in love, one that she was growing out of. She also knew that in Devon, she would find what her heart had been searching for. In Devon, she would discover her soul mate.

If she would allow the relationship to take hold of her, she knew she could never give it back, and it would destroy her.

The feelings he inspired in her were like none she had felt with Augustus, even from the start. She had thought Augustus was meant for her; she could even recall telling him so, but this, the jolt she felt when she touched Devon's hand and wrapped her own around it, couldn't be mistaken. She loved him, but she would never betray her head and speak the words.

For with certainty, on so many levels, she knew her admission of Devon's love would come at a price.

A cost too deadly to pay.

Those bare feet and stairs riddled her mind, stealing her breath.

"That's it." She whispered the words aloud. "That's what my fate is." She pushed herself up from the sandy ground and turned to Devon with wide, horrified eyes.

"What's it? What are you talking about?" Devon rose to

meet her.

"That dream, the one I told you about." Her focus widened and narrowed until she wobbled on her feet. She raised a hand to hold on to Devon before she collapsed right before him.

"Yes, I remember. What—are you okay?" Devon asked, holding her up.

She swallowed hard and attempted to clear her head, stand on her own. She clasped her hands in her pockets and felt her breathing slow until it was steady enough to tell him her worst fears, to voice the horrifying notion aloud.

"You and I, we're meant to be together. I feel it."

The quick release of breath from Devon caused her to wince. Judging from the smile spread across his face, he must have thought she was giving in to him—and their fate.

"Oh, Adelia. I know, I feel it, too." He locked eyes with her. "Now go ahead and do it. Do what we both know you need to do. Then we can be together."

"No, you're not letting me finish." She attempted to speak, but his hopeful eyes gave her pause. She had worded this all wrong, gotten his hopes up. "Devon. Yes, you and I both feel this impossible bond, but I can't—that's not all—there's more." She struggled to get her words out.

"I'm listening, Adelia. I'm listening."

"That dream, that ominous, horrendous dream—it's me. *I'm* the one falling down the stairs to meet my death."

"Huh?" He didn't understand.

"My destiny—my fate?"

"Yes? Yes?"

She paused, hating to hear the words that would come out of her mouth next. She bit back the tears and continued. "Devon?"

He didn't speak, but in his eyes she saw the worry and confusion.

She was going to break his heart.

She was going to break her own heart.

But she knew what she feared most was the truth—knew the timeline of events which had transpired would continue, play out until the bitter end. Meeting Augustus, coming to the island, and ultimately meeting Devon, all served a purpose to her destination. It hadn't been an accident that Devon had gotten lost that night and knocked upon their door.

She said the words again, this time louder, with determination. "My destiny, my fate, is to die by the hands of Augustus."

His mouth dropped as he shook his head. "No, you're talking nonsense, Adelia. It's not true. It's a dream, just a damn dream!"

She knew he was wrong, and based on Devon's outburst, he believed her as well. His own heart betrayed his words as he sank to the ground, clutching her knees.

"It's me. I'm the woman with the bare feet, and he's going to push me down those stairs." Her voice shook, breaking in tempo with her heart. "He's going to find out about the feelings we share. He'll see it in my eyes—my own heart will double-cross me—and he's going to kill me."

CHAPTER TWELVE
2017

Since that night, weeks ago, Hope and Clooney had been inseparable. It didn't matter that they rarely left the grounds of the lighthouse, as her fear for wandering off the property grew worse. She was happy—*they* were happy. That's all that mattered.

Tracy, however, felt differently, and voiced her opinion on the subject as often as she could. "I don't get it, that's all I'm saying. I mean, if he was good for you, wouldn't your agoraphobia be improving instead of growing worse?"

One would think so, but wasn't the important thing that Hope was happy? That after searching for many years, she finally found the one she was meant to be with?

"I'm happy, Tracy. Be happy for me. Can you do that?"

"I'm trying, Hope. God, I'm trying."

"It's as if we were destined to be together. I found my soul mate, and I'm not going to worry about the other thing.

It will come, if I'm meant to get better and face my fears, it will happen. Just give me the time to enjoy my life, and then maybe I'll heal."

"First off, I could understand that, but you're getting *worse*, Hope, you're getting so much *worse.*"

Hope opened her mouth to argue, but then clamped her lips shut. It was true. The magnetic pull to the lighthouse and bluffs was undeniable—it seemed the lighthouse and she were in a constant struggle, and Hope had finally surrendered. As if the building had won. An uncomfortable twinge hit her gut, and she shifted on her feet.

"And all this talk of soul mates and destiny? What the hell is that all about? You met a guy, Hope. You met a *guy*. It happens every day, and yes, I'm sure you think you're in love with him—"

"I *am* in love with him, and you know what? That shouldn't bother you. It's like one day you just woke up and decided you didn't like him. What happened?"

Her friend grew pensive, then stood up and walked over toward the kitchen sink, putting distance between herself and Hope.

Hope's hand dove into her pocket, searching out the white stone. Her throat tightened as she forced herself to take a steady breath.

"It was that—what you're doing right now." Tracy closed the space between them and threw a finger in Hope's direction. "That day at the pub when I ran into you talking to Clooney at the bar." Tracy set her jaw in determination. "He did that thing—you know, you told me that your mother used to trace her fingers on your open palm to calm you, similar to you touching that stone."

Her mother used to do just that before the stone even.

She knew it soothed Hope, and when her mother had found that white stone, she had given it to Hope and told her to touch it and it would remind her to calm down and to relax.

"So what? Why would that bother you?"

"Did you tell him about that? I mean, you had only recently met him back then."

"No, as a matter of fact, I didn't. He knows now, but not back then. But hey, that's kind of what I mean. Doesn't that tell you he and I were meant to find one another? He *gets* me, Tracy. He *gets* me. Why can't you be happy for me?"

"Does he know about the dream, too?"

"Well, yes." She saw the doubt in her friend's eyes. Before Clooney, Tracy had been the only other one to know about the nightmare and the visions. The only other person she would have trusted with the information would have been her mother. But her mother had passed awhile back. Hazy confusion pressed at her head, causing Hope to clarify the fact that her mother was, indeed, deceased. Recently, she had remembered thinking that her mother would worry for her being isolated here on the island. Shaking her head, Hope grew concerned that she had nearly forgotten the important fact. What was going on with her lately? She needed to focus and clear the clutter from her mind.

"I don't like this. It's—"

Too much, too soon?

Was Clooney playing her, using her until someone better came along?

Hope could practically read Tracy's thoughts. Is that why Tracy worried for her? "He's not a player. He won't hurt me."

Tracy shook her head. "I don't think he's a player. It's not that. It's a bit creepy, that's all, you know, how close you've become in such a short time and the dark cloud that's come over you."

"Stop saying that. I'm happier than I've ever been."

"Even if it means you're regressing? I mean, how does he stand it? Doesn't he want to go out, do normal things?"

A shudder stopped Hope cold, and she glared at her friend. A feeling Hope couldn't name washed over her, pressing her down. Tracy's words were unkind, but it was more than that. Hope was forced to admit she liked having Clooney there at the house, all to herself most of the time.

She didn't wish to share him with anyone else. The thought erupted from her mind, and then she squashed it.

Don't bring him down with you.

The prison, prison, prison.

No, this was ridiculous. Hope cleared her head, washing the bitterness from her mind. She simply enjoyed having him there with her, and he had no complaints. Why did Tracy insist upon trying to ruin this? Was she jealous that Clooney intruded upon their own time together, their friendship? Did having Clooney underfoot bother Tracy?

"Your words are cruel, Tracy."

Tracy sighed. "I'm sorry. Listen, maybe my words were harsh, but I'm only trying to get you to step outside of yourself and see the big picture."

She remained firm. "I think it would be best if we have a break from one another. Clooney is cutting out of work early tonight to be with me, and it's probably for the best that you don't run into him."

Tracy shook her head. "A break? We live together, Hope. This is my house, too!" But she walked forward, heading for her bedroom. She paused and turned to face Hope. "You know what? You're right. I'm going to stay at Tommy's for a night or two. I just hope you wake up and get out of your own way."

Hope glared at Tracy, her chest thumping. "I am awake. I'm wide awake."

Minutes after Tracy left, Hope hung her head in her hands. She felt bad. Okay, she felt horrible. The way she had behaved, telling Tracy to leave her own home, had been inexcusable. Sure, she was pissed that her friend had butted her nose into her business, but Hope knew she could have handled herself differently. Tomorrow, when Tracy was at work with her, she would apologize first thing, tell her to come home.

This year, Hope had to admit, was the first tourist season she could remember feeling so . . . blah. Normally, she thrived on the interaction she experienced with the energetic visitors. Now, all she wished to do was get the day over with and settle in with Clooney. Damn, maybe she *was* getting too close, too soon. But Hope also knew she wouldn't change a thing, right now she would ride out this surge at any cost.

A sudden knock on her door jarred the thoughts from her mind. It must be Clooney. She perked up, knowing he was on the other side of the door. As she made her way to let Clooney in, Hope contemplated sharing how Tracy felt about their relationship, but then reconsidered, not wanting to cause a rift between the only two close friends she had.

As usual, Clooney offered up his bright smile, and she ached to freeze that moment.

Almost as if he would be torn from her at some point in the near future.

She was being ridiculous, of course. But then, the all too familiar vision pummeled her again: bare feet, the lighthouse stairs . . .

That's it. Why hadn't she thought to do this before?

"Hope? Are you okay?" He leaned in, his eyes squinting.

"Come, sit down." Hope pulled him by the hand, past the entrance and into the kitchen. "I have to talk to you about something—it's important." She spoke as she led him to the table.

Clooney sat across from Hope and placed his hands in front of him, waiting for her. "What is it? You've got me worried."

"No, no need to worry. But listen—remember the dream I told you about? The visions?"

He scrunched his brow, leaning in closer. "Of course. What about them?"

"Do you know much about the history here?"

"You mean the history of the island?"

"Not quite. More specifically, the history of this lighthouse."

She watched as he pondered the question then shook his head. "Not really. I haven't been here nearly as long as you have. Although, I suppose I decided to move here because of the history my distant relatives have had on the island."

"What do you mean?" He hadn't mentioned this before. She would have remembered this.

"My grandparents, great-grandparents, and beyond were known to come here to vacation during the summers."

"Huh. Why didn't you tell me this before?"

"I guess it didn't come up."

"Okay, so I wonder if your parents, grandparents, maybe, would know about the history here."

"Well, my great-grandparents, and grandparents for that matter, have passed, and all I know from my parents is that our family had roots here way back when."

"Roots? What kind of roots?"

He shook his head and then reached for her hands across the table. "I don't know. If I remember correctly, my great-great-grandfather—or even further back, maybe it was— may have lived here briefly. It's foggy. Why does any of this matter?"

She supposed it didn't, but now she realized just how little she actually knew about Clooney. She made a mental note to discuss that with him at another time. Right now, she needed to zero in on her purpose for asking about his knowledge of the lighthouse in the first place.

"It doesn't, not really. I suppose I just figured out you and I have so much to share with each other, but that's for another time. I need to find out what really happened here at this lighthouse."

He scratched at his head and glanced around the room. "I'm not following."

'The dreams—they have to mean something." Yes, she had first considered that those bare feet belonged to her, but what if it were something else entirely?

"It can't be coincidence." There. She said it. Now that the words were spoken aloud, her convictions felt stronger. The setting of those visions clearly took place in her lighthouse, and now she felt it in her bones—something awful.

Something horrible had happened here. Right here. And it must have been so awful that the walls, the heart of the building just couldn't let it go. Never one to put much thought into ghosts or spirits before, the sudden shiver that coursed through her veins forced her to consider the possibility.

"I still don't follow. Are you saying that someone was murdered here? Next door in the *lighthouse?*" Clooney's eyes grew wide as he gestured in the direction of her cherished Amity Lighthouse.

She stood to pace the floor. With each step, the possibility seemed to spin into an almost certainty. Yes—instead of it being her, it had to be some other woman in her dreams with the bare feet, and she was definitely pushed down those stairs. It was as if someone was attempting to tell her something, but what?

If only she could see the face of the person who had pushed her. If she tried hard, really hard, to concentrate the next time she dreamt, could Hope discover more? Dreaming had never worked that way with her in the past, and she was yet to have a lucid dream, but she could try.

"Yes. I think that's exactly what I'm saying." Nodding her head, Hope felt strongly about her beliefs.

"Well, I don't even know how to respond to this. When? When could this have happened?"

She grabbed her stone and then sighed, dropping the stone and taking her hands out of her pockets and placing them on her aching head. It was too much information, her senses were on overload.

"I don't know, Clooney. I have no idea. I have to process all of this and try to make sense of it." Her skull pounded, each throb zapping more of her strength and energy.

"How long have *you* lived here?" He pressed her arm, seeking a response she couldn't give. "Hope? How long?"

"I can't think right now. My head hurts." Her thoughts tossed and tumbled. It had been a few years, or maybe more? The stress of seeing those bare feet, those stairs, feeling herself tumble . . . but it wasn't her that fell; no, it only felt that way in her dreams.

Could she help this faceless woman? Was that the reason she was plagued by these dreams night and day? Maybe it was her purpose to right a wrong, set the record straight for this crime.

"Hope? Hope?"

"Stop talking, Clooney. *Stop talking*." She hadn't intended to hurt his feelings, but based on his ensuing silence, she knew she had. If only she could stop the incessant pounding, and his chatter for that matter—then she could think more clearly, sort some of this out. "Stop talking!"

Glancing up from the fog in her mind, Hope saw the pain in his eyes. "I'm sorry. My head is throbbing, and all of this . . . stuff . . . just came at me all at once."

He attempted to smile, but his grin didn't reach his eyes. "No, I get it. No worries."

Releasing a deep breath, she felt her shoulders fall slightly. There, that was better. She could almost see the cobwebs clearing out the important information from the clutter in her mind. "I really am sorry. I don't know what's gotten into me lately." First Tracy, then Clooney. She considered that after spending so much time on her own, she made for a pretty terrible friend.

"I said it's okay. Listen, I get that you're upset about this dream thing, and I don't want to piss you off any more. So how about this? When you feel like talking about it, just do. Otherwise, I'll leave it alone."

"Clooney, I think we should talk with someone down at the town clerk's office to see what we can find out about the previous owners and lighthouse keepers." She closed her eyes tightly and tried to block out any outside distractions.

She already knew Tracy hadn't witnessed anything out of the ordinary. Why was she the one who got the privilege of having to see these visions?

Something told her that if this crime did indeed occur, it was a long time ago. Was it the walls, the chipped paint that adorned the lighthouse? Presently, the paint crumbled as the stairs narrowed to the tower; it was to be considered part of its charm, she had been told, so it would make sense that the better shape the paint was in, the farther back this went in time, but that was just a theory. Was the paint peeling off in her visions? She couldn't remember.

Damn, she couldn't remember.

But something else hung so close she could almost grab it—another clue about the time period? With each moment she strained her brain to remember, her throbbing headache increased in intensity.

Then it came to her. In a rapid flash, she was able to pull the image from her dream. She could just make out a long, white dress with some type of lacy pattern—and it appeared dirty—above the bare feet. Then the picture in her head disappeared, but in its wake, it left a trace of possibility.

"The woman, she was wearing a long dress, like something from many, many years ago."

"Okay, so at least we have a plan. Now, the next step would be to take a trip into town to find out more." Clooney's eyes drifted to the ground as he spoke.

That would entail leaving the property. She glanced out the window and then felt Clooney's hand close around hers. "I'll be there with you. Don't you know by now that I won't let anything happen to you?"

"You won't?"

"Not if I can help it." Somehow his last words weren't

exactly reassuring, but she knew he was trying to help her.

Better to be honest than tell a lie.

Now where had that come from? The past few days, phrases, not unlike the one she just thought, seemed to be passed to her; from where, she had no idea—but how could that be, and what did they even mean? Maybe it all meant that she was losing touch with reality, a thought too distressful to consider.

What was she afraid of? God, if only she could articulate, even to herself, what she feared by leaving the property. If she could only pinpoint the source of her distress.

If anyone came out and asked what she was afraid of, Hope could only answer with what she felt: it wasn't specific in nature, more vague than anything. Almost as if something—an unidentified *something*—would reach out and take hold of her, squeeze the life out of her.

Even worse, you could lose Clooney somehow.

"I think we could probably figure this out just as well through some phone calls."

"I doubt that, but I can't force you to go." Disappointment played over his features.

"You can't. Let's make the phone calls."

"That's not the way to do it. Listen, let's sit down and make a list, and then I'll go ahead into town tomorrow before work and see what I can find out on my own."

The thought of him wandering around town, asking questions with or without her, caused a wrenching in her gut. "No, I can't ask you to do that. It's my problem."

He sat before her and smoothed his hair. "It's *our* problem, Hope, and I don't mind. Whatever this is that's haunting you day and night is *our* problem."

Her heart opened up for him even more at that moment.

"I love you, Clooney." They had said the words to each other before, and it felt so good to say them again.

Like a normal couple.

But you're not normal.

She didn't flinch. This moment would not be ruined.

"I love you too, baby." He squeezed her in his arms and released a deep breath. "Now let's do this. Do you have a pen and paper?"

She excused herself before returning to the table with a pen and pad of paper.

He grinned at her and straightened his back. "Where do we start?"

"I don't want you to go without me. When I'm ready, we'll go together," she lied, knowing that after they brainstormed the list of questions, she would make some phone calls by herself the next day. Even the idea of talking to people over the phone stirred unease in Hope, but it was better than the alternative.

"Okay, if that's what you really want." He studied her intently. "But Hope?"

"What is it?"

"I'd like you to come down to the pub tomorrow to visit me." He paused, but then continued on. "It would mean the world to me."

Shaking her head, she bit down on her lip. She thought he understood what she was going through. "No, I'm not up to it."

Sadness hit his eyes. "It's getting worse, Hope. I can see it, and I feel so damn frustrated that I don't know how to help you."

She turned her face from him and wished she could promise him she would make that visit to see him at work tomorrow.

But she couldn't, and for that matter, each night when it came time to say goodbye, the unwelcome intruder that claimed her own freedom whispered in her ear to keep Clooney close—closer than ever, or she might just lose him forever. Tonight, with Tracy out of the house, she needed him more than ever.

"Stay the night, Clooney? Stay with me?" Her hands reached for him and clutched tightly. For the briefest of moments, she saw his hesitation. But then it was gone, replaced by kindness in his warm eyes.

"Okay, Hope. But I have things to do in the morning before work, so I'll have to leave early."

She was glad that she had him until the sun rose to welcome a new day. Hope jumped up and grabbed two wineglasses and a bottle of their favorite red. Uncorking the wine, she kept her eyes steadily on Clooney, who couldn't remove the coy grin playing on his face. This would be the first night they would spend together, and if she wasn't mistaken, it was to be an evening of another first endeavor with him.

CHAPTER THIRTEEN
1876

"THIS IS NONSENSE, Adelia. Yes, I believe you are in danger with the state that your husband is in, but I don't think your dream is a premonition of things to come. I won't allow myself to think such a thing."

She knew it was true; to her, there could be no other explanation. The question was, did she have the power to change her fate? Since the idea had come to pass, Adelia must have wrapped her head around her short-term plan countless times. This could work—she was sure of it. Adelia was given the gift of the premonition for a reason. As surely as her destiny was wrapped in that vision, so was the dream. The dream had been handed to her as part of her fate, and yes, she had to believe it held the power to change the outcome of her ultimate destination in this world; otherwise, what a cruel trick of nature it would be to give her this sight and withhold the power to change anything.

"It's true, Devon; it's all true. But we can work around this. I think I changed my fate by seeing what my future could be."

"You're not making sense, Adelia. What are you talking about?"

"I'm *saying* that we stopped whatever could have happened before it actually happened. I think. I hope." Although, Adelia knew in her heart she couldn't ever be with another man when she had a husband at home, however warped his mind had become. It just made the premonition even more baffling.

Devon's face darkened. "I still don't like it. I'll say it again. I don't think you're safe."

And this doesn't change the feelings we have that we can never act on. The words were forefront on her mind. Could they still be friends?

"Devon. Before I started to tell you all of this, there was something I wanted to say. Something very important." She stopped to look at him for a quick moment, then glanced around, afraid she would lose her courage. What she had to say couldn't wait. She would lose her one and only friend here on this island. Knowing Devon, she figured he wouldn't come around to see Augustus after she had this conversation with him, but nonetheless, she needed to say the words.

The wind picked up and Adelia knew she was on borrowed time. It wouldn't be good for Augustus to come down those horrid steps looking to see what was for dinner and find her missing. Closing her eyes, Adelia grasped hold of Devon's hand and began.

"Devon, you've been my saving grace up here on the bluffs. You've touched my life and made it so much better. I'm proud to call you my friend." The next part would be the hardest.

"Please, I know what you're going to say, Adelia. I know—I just don't want to hear it."

"You *need* to hear it. *I* need to say it." He had to stop interrupting her, or she'd never have a chance to say those words she needed to get out of her head. Out of her head, yes, but never out of her heart.

Adelia opened her mouth to finish, but Devon pressed a single finger to her lips. "Shh—can you do me one last favor?"

He was infuriating. The words were hard enough to say aloud, but worse when he kept stopping her train of thought. *Stop talking, let me finish.*

"What, Devon? What is it?" She tapped her foot on the sand below instead of yelling the words that were on her mind.

"I know we can't be friends anymore. I knew it before you even mentioned the connection between your dream and what you allow yourself to believe is to be your fate."

She considered interrupting him, to correct him and tell him that the dream *was* her fate, but decided, unlike him, she would not interrupt and therefore let him continue.

"It's why I feel the way I do about you. You're a unique soul, and I respect you for both your honesty and your integrity. If and when you ever find yourself apart from Augustus, you can search me out." He lingered on the last words for a moment. "I can't make any promises that I'll wait forever, because Adelia, I'm only a living, breathing man. But I can promise you that you will forever hold a piece of my heart."

Now she couldn't interrupt if she tried. Tears glistened in his eyes as she swiped away her own. He was a good man.

Of course he would get on with his life; he deserved nothing less, and she wished him all the happiness in the world.

"But, my sweet Adelia—" He spoke her name deliberately, and it struck her that her name coming from his lips sounded as if it was a flower. She had never heard her name spoken so delicately, and like a petal, she would eventually wither away without his companionship. It was the price she had to pay to save both herself and Augustus.

"What is it?" she squeaked, not taking her eyes from his face.

"I can't stay here on the island." He blurted out the words and hung his head.

"What? Why not?" What had she expected, and what difference would it ultimately make? It wasn't as if they could see each other.

"This was only meant to be a temporary stay. I'm an explorer at heart and only planned on staying less than a year to begin with. When I met you, I considered prolonging my visit on the island." He cleared his throat and gathered himself together. "But know that I would have stayed here with you forever, had it been possible."

What did he expect her to say? Did he want her to beg? It was out of her hands now, her new fate sealed in her mind. "Devon."

"I know, I know. I'll leave come Wednesday, first thing in the morning. I've already arranged the boat trip south."

South of here? Where was he going next? Forget it—she didn't even want to know.

"Wednesday? But tomorrow is Tuesday!" Her mind flew to their daily walks, their late night meetings on the bluffs, the dinners at the house. She would go back to being on her own with no one to speak to but a man who was growing madder by the day.

She was in this alone now. She tightened up her next course of action in her head. It was the only thing to do to keep from facing the reality before her. Yes, she would speak to the doctor tomorrow first thing. She would have to figure out the best time to walk into town without Augustus noticing.

"Adelia, did you hear what I said?"

"Wednesday morning, you'll leave at first light," she managed.

"Yes, I'm afraid so. It's for the best. If I stay any longer, I'll go crazy with worry about you, and I might just go up to that damn tower and strangle him."

"Don't say that. Not even in jest." Her mind went to a horrible place. The last thing she needed was more images she had to block out.

"If I ever find out that he hurts you, I'll kill him. I swear on my life I will."

She worried that he actually might and felt saddened about the whole state of affairs and what her life had become. Not so long ago, she had been a happy bride, looking forward to spending her life with her husband and having her first child of many. Then came another flash, the recent image Adelia had experienced. She recalled the momentary relief, guilt, and freedom she felt as she imagined Augustus stumbling down the steps after losing his footing, his glass of gin in hand. How had she gotten to this dark place?

Sighing, Adelia prayed for some answers, and she knew that at least for now, they could only come from the doctor. It was the only chance she had at repairing not only her marriage, but her husband's sanity—and possibly her own.

"Don't say things that could cause you to wind up locked

away forever, Devon." She gazed into the depths of his eyes and then closed her own, imprinting his face in her heart and mind.

"Could you do me one last favor?"

"I believe I can. What is it?"

"You have a lot to mull over and need to prepare for your trip to the doctor tomorrow."

She nodded, hoping the doctor would agree to speak with her on such short notice. Waiting for Devon to continue, she took his hands and placed them in hers. She would do what he asked, after all, and he knew it.

"Meet me here, on top of the bluffs, tomorrow night. As soon as Augustus passes out from his drink, come here to say goodbye."

She nodded, blinking away fresh tears. She would do that for him. He deserved a proper exit. It would sting terribly, seeing him that one last time, but she would summon her strength.

He squeezed her hands and then cursed as he released her and then pressed her close once more.

When he finally broke free from her, he took the first step to walk away. "Until tomorrow, Adelia." He waved his hand as he disappeared into the brush.

Adelia raised her own hand in response. "Until tomorrow," she whispered as she watched him disappear from sight.

CHAPTER FOURTEEN
2017

Lying next to Clooney in her bed, she kissed his face, neck, and chest, touching every exposed inch of him. She wished to claim him as her own. Her raw nerves ached to touch him, *devour* him. *Slow down. Take it easy.* If she wasn't careful, she just might scare him off. She opened her eyes to gaze up at his equally matched passion and concluded she had nothing to worry about. Clooney was in as deep as she was. She buried herself in the warmth of his body and took hold of his arms. She held on tighter, closing her eyes to savor the deliciousness of the moment.

"You're so beautiful, I can't tear my eyes away from you." His eyes wandered about her face, then his mouth melted down to explore her lips, chin, and neck. Never before had anyone called her beautiful; cute, maybe, and she had been fine with that. She was no raving beauty, and it had never mattered. Hearing the words spout from Clooney's mouth, she knew she had been waiting to hear those words, not just her whole life, but from him.

"Clooney." All she could see, taste, and smell was him. *Clooney.* "Tell me you love me," she ordered, her tone growing insistent. "Tell me."

He growled her name, saying it over and over. "Hope."

"Say it—say the words I need to hear." Her head pounded, suddenly frantic, desperate to hear him proclaim his love for her. Why couldn't he just say it? She felt her temperature rise and bit back another demand.

"Hope—"

"Tell me!" she bellowed, then cringed, hating the way her rising hysteria sounded, even to her own ears.

He pressed kisses all over her face, saying her name again and again until she felt as if she would burst.

Say the words. Just say the freaking words.

"I love you, Hope." His eyes met hers, and she let her rigid body relax, sighing a breath of relief. Only when he finally uttered those words did she give herself permission to relax.

Once the moment passed, she cringed at her sudden forcefulness with Clooney. Never before had she been so bold as to shout out a command like that; never before had she felt such fear at losing someone if he didn't prove that he loved her.

The possibility of losing him, the thought of being all alone up here on the bluff when Tracy left, scared the hell out of her. Now that she tasted what life with someone else—life with Clooney—felt like, there was no going back.

"I'm sorry, Clooney."

He ran his fingers across her belly. "For what?"

"You know . . . for being so outspoken." She waited for

his response.

His fingers came to a halt as he stopped tracing circles on her stomach. "Hope, I thought you were very sexy. I love that direct side of you, and as a mater of fact, I wish I saw more of it."

Oh. "Really?" She fought past the shame of her recent behavior and looked him directly in the eye. "It wasn't too much?"

"No. It was perfect. It was *you.*" He kissed her tenderly and then nibbled on her bottom lip. "Come here, you. I love your lips. They're so soft and full." She tore away, focused on what he had said moments before.

It was you.

But that was the problem. It *wasn't* Hope. She wasn't the brazen type and could hardly believe her boldness. The moment had swept over her, controlling her thoughts and senses—like she was given no choice—then it was gone, and she was left reeling with embarrassment and confusion. Chalk it up to the fact that she had never been in love before; maybe it was only her immaturity as being part of a couple.

"And I do love you. That's one thing you don't need to question, Hope, ever." He took her hand and placed a solid kiss on it, squashing away any worries.

"Good. That's good, Clooney." She loosened the knot she had formed with her fingers.

He stretched his arms over his head and yawned. "As much as I'd love to spend the rest of the night talking with you, I have to get some sleep."

Although Hope knew she wouldn't sleep a wink, she kissed him good night and cuddled up against him. Instead of enjoying the feel of Clooney's warm body beside hers, Hope worried about the nights she would be here without him. He wouldn't stay every night, even though that was her greatest wish right now.

Don't let him go. Don't let him leave.

She blinked her eyes shut, blocking out the thoughts. She needed to get some rest. Sleep had never come easily for Hope as she always had so much on her mind. If she could just find an off switch, she might rest. There was no such switch for her, and after hearing Clooney's soft sighs of slumber, Hope closed her eyes tight, willing the darkness to envelop her.

The vision hit her with such ferocity, she cried out. Those feet, the bare feet that taunted her, now lay lifeless on the bottom of the lighthouse steps, bent at an unnatural angle with the dress riding up her ankle.

Go away.

Go away.

Go away.

Hope bit down so hard on her lip, she felt the warm blood seep into her mouth, tasted the salty bitterness. Then, a scream and yet another voice called out. She couldn't detect each word, for the bellowing came at her as if from the distance. A hollow, eerie cry called out, something about *his house. He made this house—blood, sweat, tears.*

He built the house.

"Clooney!" Hope sat up in a flash, sweat pooling over her chest. "Clooney!" She grabbed hold of him, shaking him furiously.

"What is it?" he responded, trying to get his bearings about him. "What happened?"

"I saw it—the vision, but this time—" She began shaking, her hands trembling uncontrollably until Clooney did what he did best: soothed her.

"It's okay, I'm here. Slow down, just slow down." He ran a steady hand over her skin, reaching down for her palm, circling his fingers on her palm over and over. "You okay?"

She swallowed, gathering up her strength to continue. "I—it was worse. I saw more, heard more this time. Clooney, she was dead, the woman with the bare feet, she had to be. I know it, and then there were voices—men, I think. I'm not sure how many there were, it was so hard to tell." Her voice shook with fear.

"It's okay, I have you. You don't have to tell me everything right now." He pressed his fingers over hers.

"No, I have to. I don't want to forget a thing. Her feet were bent, and she wasn't moving. There was the dirt-stained dress I saw the last time and the man was saying something. He said something." She paused, straining to recall his exact words. "He said he made the house—built it with his own blood, sweat, tears . . ."

What sense did any of this make, and why would he proclaim that instead of running to the bottom of the stairs to try to help the poor woman? Unless . . .

"I'll go. I'll go with you tomorrow."

Clooney shook his head and stared at her. "Where? Where am I going tomorrow?"

How could he forget what they had discussed earlier? "Clooney, I'm going into town tomorrow, even if it kills me. I don't think we're dealing with an accident here. I think those feet, that woman—was murdered."

CHAPTER FIFTEEN
2017

Tᴙᴜᴇ ᴛᴏ ʜᴇʀ word, she woke early the next morning. Scratch that, she got out of bed early. Sleep hadn't come to her at all, what with the morbid vision and Clooney lying next to her. How could she have possibly slept?

Clooney had grabbed a cup of coffee from her and rushed out, telling Hope he would be back in an hour or two to grab her. She had better not lose her courage, Hope told herself as she sipped at her own coffee. Each time she felt herself waning, all she needed to do was bring forth the image of that twisted foot and the male voice. She had to be brave and start investigating what actually took place in her own backyard, years earlier.

"Where the hell are you? Clooney, where are you?" Anxiety covered her chest, squashing down, swallowing her as a thought erupted.

What if he doesn't come back for you?

What if he's had enough?
What if, what if . . .

"Stop it. Stop!" She held her head in her hands, mentally sweeping the words from her mind.

Hope's eyes wandered to the clock on her kitchen wall, and she winced. He had only been gone less than an hour. Less than an hour, and here she was getting hysterical. As quickly as the uncomfortable feeling had come over her, it was gone, now replaced with a sense of calm. Hope was clearly inexperienced in the ways of men and relationships, and these irrational feelings had to end. She felt up, down, and everywhere in between.

It ended up that Hope didn't need to wait long for Clooney to return for her. As happy as she was to see him, she couldn't squash the uneasy feeling she had tried so hard to bury minutes earlier. She didn't want to rely on someone so desperately that she couldn't be happy anymore without him by her side. She made a mental note to give herself a little distance from him today, if not physically, then at least mentally. She needed to prove to herself that if something happened and their relationship didn't pan out, she would be okay on her own.

"Ready, beautiful?" He rushed over, bumping into her as she nearly spilled her coffee.

"Yes. Just give me a minute, please." She returned his kiss, trying not to notice how damn good he smelled. He smelled like Clooney: fresh, a hint of soap, spice.

What are you going to do without him?
What are you going to do when you're all alone?
Tracy's leaving, too. They all end up leaving you.
Every. Single. One.

She wouldn't break. She would not break.

"Everything okay?" He stepped back and studied her.

"Sure, yes." Clearing her throat, she raised a finger, signaling that she would return in a moment. Hope hurried to her bedroom where she clutched her bedpost, gripping her fingers into the wood. Maybe she needed therapy. She had been single for so long, she couldn't bear the thought of being on her own again if this didn't work out. What she didn't need, on top of those horrid visions, were these intrusive, sudden bursts of negative, damaging thoughts hell-bent on pulling her down.

Swiping at her face, Hope then walked over to her dresser to grab her bag. What would Tracy tell her now? Well, she and Tracy weren't exactly on the best of terms, but she hoped that would be rectified as soon as she saw her friend at work later. Now, she had to get back out there to Clooney.

He stood, sunlight streaming through his wavy hair, his eyes warm. A familiar tug pulled at her, like they had been doing this forever. Clooney could have any woman he desired, and yet, here he stood with her. Right now, instead of the worry she normally felt, she felt lucky and scoffed at the idea of giving herself some space from him.

"Let's do this."

"Yes." Before she even allowed that slice of apprehension to cut through her, Hope brought forth the image of those feet at the bottom of the stairs—the stairs at *her* lighthouse—and held her head high. She had a larger purpose here, and she wouldn't be dragged down by her own insecurities.

"You okay?" Clooney stepped out into the bright morning sunlight with her. Looking at the cloudless sky overhead and hearing the birds chirping, she figured it was a sign that she was doing the right thing by taking the first baby step to clearing the visions and possibly sweeping away her own musty cobwebs in the process.

"Where to first?" He grabbed her hand and smiled down at her.

"Historical society. I think picking the brains of people who thrive in the history of this town is as good a place to start as any." Then maybe the town clerk's office, Chamber of Commerce, library.

"Sure thing." He opened the passenger side door to his car for her and then walked around to settle in beside her.

"I'm proud of you." He glanced at her before putting his sunglasses on.

"Don't get all gooey on me, let's just do this before I chicken out." The more Hope thought about what she was doing, the more she knew the chances for panic mode, as she named it, would come calling.

Comfortable silence filled the air as they made a turn out of the lot and onto the main road. Her heart picked up a notch, and she squashed it back down with some more of the disturbing images from the past. At one point, Clooney reached to turn the radio on, and she winced, asking him to shut it off. She needed a clear, steady mind with no conversation or music to muddle her thoughts. When they finally pulled over in front of the historical society, Hope sucked in her breath and counted to ten, then made it twenty before she released her hand from the stone in her pocket.

"Are you sure——"

What the hell was the matter with him? Didn't Clooney understand that giving her the chance to back out, she just might?

"Shut *up*." She blurted out the words before she could think. "Sorry." Sheepishly, Hope glanced at Clooney and squeezed his hand. She reined in her temper and hoped he would understand.

"I get it."

Good.

From the car window, Hope gazed out at the old, white Dutch Colonial that housed the museum. She would venture to guess that it had been built sometime in the 1800s.

He opened his mouth to say something, but then closed it. He took a moment to stare at her before he turned off the ignition. "Come on."

Stepping in time with Clooney, Hope stuck one hand in her pocket, and the other hand wrapped around Clooney's arm. From the few cars in the parking area, it looked as if the small museum wasn't too crowded.

"Welcome." An older brunette woman ushered them inside once they opened the door. She appeared to be friendly enough, which was exactly what they needed today.

"Hi, I'm hoping you can help us answer some questions." Clooney introduced himself as Hope stood back, praying she had the strength to stay by his side and not hightail it back to the car.

The woman glanced at them and then cleared her throat. "Nice to meet you. I'm so glad you could stop by to visit our town and the museum here."

"Oh, we're not visitors. I moved here recently and Hope has lived here for a long time," Clooney explained.

The woman scratched her head and gazed in Hope's direction, her eyes widening. There it was again, the odd stare. Hope swallowed back her own greeting, fearful that her shaking voice would scare the woman off even more.

"Yes, what can I do for you?"

"Surely you must have made a trip up to the lighthouse on the bluffs. Hope works there giving tours and overseeing the property." Clooney grabbed hold of her hand as he spoke, pulling her forward just a bit.

Hope plastered on a smile. "Yes, I've been there a while. Have you had the opportunity to come by and check out the lighthouse?"

Hope went into her work mode talk, hoping it would calm her before she reconsidered this whole plan and just turned around and went home.

"I—uh." The woman glanced down at the floor, seemingly distracted. It was hard, just so damn *hard* to do this, make conversation with people who treated her as if she had the plague. Did she look so freaking strange to people? Hope didn't think so, but then what the hell was it?

Clooney interjected, clearly trying to rescue her. "What did you say your name was, miss?"

"Jane. I'm Jane Everett."

As sweet as he was, she didn't need Clooney to save her from this conversation; she just wasn't prepared to answer questions about why most people in town wouldn't recognize her. Given the fact that she rarely made it into town, it was no shock Jane didn't know who she was.

"Jane, you must have met one of the other employees at the lighthouse. Her name is Tracy," Hope interjected.

Jane scrunched her nose, still silent.

"Dark hair, late twenties?" Clooney offered up at bit more information.

"Who?" Jane tilted her chin, her eyes searching Clooney's face. Hope suddenly wondered if the woman might be showing some signs of dementia. It struck her as sad, the confusion that played out on Jane's features.

"The woman, Tracy, the one who works at the lighthouse," Clooney stated, his brows scrunched together.

"Yes, sure." Jane glanced at the floor and then changed the subject. Hope felt some relief now that the conversation wasn't centered around her. Then finally Clooney began asking the questions they were here for.

"Do you know much about the history of the early lighthouse keepers?"

"I know mostly everything you would need to know on the subject and what I don't, you could probably find out at the town clerk's office. Here, come with me."

Jane led them to the next level of the charming old house. Everywhere Hope turned, there was an abundance of history. Why hadn't she ventured out and visited the building before? Hope figured she could spend the entire day here and never grow tired—if she could summon up the courage, that is.

"What was that?" Hope didn't hear what Jane had said as she was caught off guard, lost in another place and time, staring at the numerous artifacts surrounding her.

"This island has so much history, you really should explore. Have you been on all of the trails? Seen all of the quaint little shops?" Jane gushed about the island, and it just served to make Hope feel bad about all of the things she hadn't yet discovered due to the limitations she placed upon herself.

"Oh. Well, honestly, I don't get out much." That certainly was no lie.

"She's kind of a homebody, focused on the business up there on the bluffs," Clooney stated, clearly attempting to lessen Hope's stress level. One thing she didn't enjoy was defending herself when it came to the amount of time she spent at home.

An odd look came over Jane's face as she turned to glance

at Clooney. Hope nudged Clooney, urging him to keep walking. They needed to get on with this visit without all of the small talk. With each exchange, Hope felt herself fade ever so slightly.

"Here. These pictures are of some of the keepers of the lighthouse and their families." Jane pointed at a series of old photographs, dating as far back as the 1800s. Some of the photographs had been preserved quite well while others were torn and faded. The glare from the display case wasn't helping matters.

"Is it possible to take these out so I can see them better?" Clooney read her mind.

Jane hesitated, then stepped behind the counter to reach for the vintage photographs.

"I'm not supposed to do this, but you seem very interested in these pictures. Just be careful please."

Photograph by photograph, Hope scrutinized each one. "It's difficult to even see their faces in some of these." Hope turned to gauge Clooney's reaction, but he appeared as stumped as she was. What was she seeking to gain by looking at these pictures anyway? All she had seen in the visions were those feet and the woman's dress. It hit her that they were asking the wrong questions.

"Jane, to your knowledge, did anything out of the ordinary ever happen to any of the keepers?" Clooney asked the questions now as Hope felt the tension of the morning seeping in. She fingered the stone in her pocket and counted to ten.

Breathe.

Breathe.

Jane opened her mouth to speak and then shut it again. "Hm. Well, there is a story about one of the early owners, but from where I stand, it's just that—a story, if you will."

"What is it? What happened?" Hope nearly lunged at Jane. She felt the reassurance of Clooney's arm grounding her.

"What happened?" Clooney repeated the question, clearly as excited as Hope was to get some answers.

"Oh, it's nonsense if you ask me." Jane waved her hand, as if dismissing the absurd thought.

Just tell me.

"Humor us," Clooney stated, more calmly than Hope could have.

Jane's gaze drifted toward Clooney for a lingering moment before resting on one particularly aged photograph. The edges were torn and the image was a faded old black and white.

Jane's finger touched the image of the man in the picture. A flash of emotion she couldn't pinpoint zapped her. She inhaled deeply to steady her nerves. As faded as the image was, the man appeared handsome, with dark hair and serious, stoic features. If Hope looked closely enough, she could almost make out something akin to joy or happiness in his eyes.

On second glance, she thought she discovered something darker in his eyes, but then it was gone.

"Hope?"

"I'm fine." She needed to figure out what it was about the photograph that sucked the breath from her.

"This here was Augustus MacGregor and his wife, Adelia. They were the second but most significant owners, in my opinion—that is, if you're looking for spooky fireside stories." She chuckled and wrapped her arms across her chest before continuing. "See Adelia here?" Jane's finger jabbed the image of the woman named Adelia. She was dressed in a modest, ankle-length dress, and her face was partially covered by a large bonnet topped by an abundance of feathers and flowers. Shade camouflaged the rest of her face.

"Hard to tell, I can barely make out her face, what with the hat and all." It was a poor quality picture, but honestly, what could you expect from such an old photo?

"What happened to her?" The words were barely out of her mouth before flashes of feet, a torn dress, and yelling tore at her. Clooney grabbed her from behind, steadying her.

"Are you okay? I hope you don't mind me saying that you don't look well."

"She's fine," Clooney stated, his arms still holding her upright. Numbness and tingling coursed through Hope's entire body, and she urged herself to breathe.

"Can I get you some water?" Jane's gaze traveled toward Clooney once more. "Is everything okay?"

"Water would be great, thank you," Clooney responded for Hope, and this time, she didn't mind. Waiting for Jane to disappear down the flight of stairs, Hope clutched on to Clooney's arm.

"It came at me hard. This has to mean something."

"Are you okay? Is this too much for you?" He leaned over, whispering in her ear.

"Are you trying to get me to crawl back into my shell and run home? With no answers?" She spat the words out, not caring right now how they sounded or if she hurt his feelings.

"No, Hope, I'm not. But judging from your pale complexion and the look in your eyes, I figured I'd ask if you needed a break." His own words were touched with annoyance. Before she could say anything, Clooney stepped away from her and ran his hands through his hair.

"Here you go. Some nice, cold water for you." Jane's entrance broke the tension in the room. She placed the water down as Clooney returned to his spot beside her.

As Clooney spoke with Jane, they made their way back to the pictures. Hope lifted the cold liquid to her lips and allowed the water to stream down to her belly, relaxing her with each gulp. Now she could see the error of her harsh words and prayed he wouldn't give up on her. If only she could control her sharp tongue and keep her negativity to herself.

"Where were we?" Hope joined them after placing her water down. She blinked her eyes and planted a smile on her face.

"Yes, please continue." Clooney wiped the sweat from his brow.

"You're sure you don't want to rest a bit?" Jane glanced at Clooney and the space where Hope stood.

"No, I'm good. What is it you were saying about these two?" Hope pointed down at the photograph and steeled herself for the possibility of being hit with another vision. Although by her side, Clooney remained silent.

"Clooney, this might be important." She would apologize later; right now she needed his perspective on what Jane was about to share.

Jane cleared her throat.

"Fine, so these two?" Clooney joined the conversation once more, gesturing toward the photograph.

"So yes, the story about these two. It is said that Augustus and Adelia were both thrown down the stairs, to their deaths, by—" Each second that Jane paused caused Hope's heart to speed up even more. Wasn't there only one pair of feet in her visions? Who had been yelling at the top of those stairs? Hope didn't need to hear the silence in Jane's dramatic pause, what she needed was answers.

Now.

Clenching her fists into tight balls, Hope knew from the tension in her body that she was about to lose it.

Strategies, Hope, count to ten.

"Adelia's secret lover." Jane clasped her hands together, a wily grin lighting up her face as if she were sharing gossip with her best girlfriend.

First, she exhaled—deeply.

Next, she grabbed for her stone.

Then, she turned to search Clooney's face.

Finally, Hope sank to her knees, allowing the release of her emotions. Clooney fell to her side in an instant, his comforting arms embracing her. Jane backed up, muttering something about getting more water. Even Hope didn't understand the reason this story had touched her so deeply.

Her fall had been a deluge of everything coming to a head—from her insecurities about Clooney, to her phobias, fear, anxiety, her argument with Tracy, the visions—then it all circled back to Clooney.

"Did you feel something?" Clooney stroked her hair, waiting out her response.

And then came the vision: the feet, stairs, and yes, a clean, fresh coat of paint on the walls.

"I felt *everything.*"

CHAPTER SIXTEEN
1876

A BLACK CAT could mean bad luck if it approached, and then again it was said to bring good luck if it walked away. She didn't believe in the nonsense and superstition stemming from the history of black cats, and more specifically, the beliefs of pirates abound. Adelia still treaded cautiously and came to a complete stop when she witnessed the cat.

What did it mean if the black cat stopped in its tracks and simply stared at you? It seemed as if they were almost in a battle of wills, but in the end, it was the cat who broke their connection with a last glance and a lift of its tail as it walked away, almost as if it, too, knew the stories about black cats and purposely chose to release her from any bad vibes.

"I'll be . . . " Adelia muttered aloud, shaking her head.

Adelia had a thought. Chuckling, she stepped up her pace. What did it mean if said cat did indeed walk away, but she went after it? She didn't care. Adelia quickened her pace, approaching fast from behind the feline. The darn cat just kept walking; she called out, but nothing. Finally, when she was directly upon the cat from behind, she reached out and lifted it.

Not knowing what to expect, she braced herself for a scratch or bite, but on the contrary, she was given a curious glance before the cat purred, cuddled close, and rewarded her with the sweet, rough texture of its little tongue.

The soft, wet kisses made her giggle, and she scooped the cat even closer. Hadn't she recently considered finding a cat? Hell, Augustus had even given his blessing on the matter—well, in a way, she supposed.

Get a cat.

She replayed his answer to her loneliness and figured she and this feline had been meant to find one another.

"Who do you belong to?" She turned the cat around, inspecting it. It appeared to be in excellent health, albeit a bit on the skinny side. "So you're a girl, are you?" She laughed as the cat placed more wet kisses on her nose.

What if it belonged to someone else, though? Knowing what she must do, Adelia gently placed the cat down on the dirt road.

She whispered softly to her. "If you follow me, we're meant to be." Adelia walked forward, daring to take a peek over her shoulder. She was delighted to see the young cat speed up and walk in time beside her.

"So it appears we're meant to be." This little visitor brightened what was otherwise a bleak, gray morning. She had succeeded in sneaking out of the house while Augustus was painting yet another fresh coat of paint on the walls of the staircase.

He was becoming increasingly obsessed with the upkeep

of the building, muttering about how well he took care of *his* house incessantly. She had the mind to smack some sense into him and cry out that it was her house, too. Didn't she keep it clean, cook the meals, wash his clothes, tend to the horses they borrowed to go into town?

She imagined herself summoning up the courage to scream the words at him. One day. *This is my house, too, Augustus. I live here, too.* Despite the troubles with her deteriorating marriage and the sickness of Augustus, she loved her house and the bluffs dearly, so much so at times, the stark beauty of her home brought tears to her eyes. The pride she felt when thinking about her home never ceased to amaze or surprise her. Most would probably despise the place where one's marriage fell apart, but Adelia knew better—it wasn't a place that drove a man and a woman apart, caused a wedge in their marriage. It was the people who did this.

Thinking again about speaking up to Augustus, she doubted the words would ever slip from her mouth, but oh, what pleasure it would give her to say those words and see the shocked expression, the rage on his face.

It's more my house than it could ever be yours.

She longed to say those words, for her connection to the lighthouse stemmed from the heart, not from some sick compulsion to own the building as if it were merely a property. The lighthouse seemed to have taken on a heart of its own, sustaining her when she needed it most, giving her the sense of security that Augustus had failed at so miserably.

"Come now." Adelia conversed with the affectionate kitty, their banter consisting of small talk on Adelia's part and soft mews from her new friend. Adelia figured she would make the trip to try to talk to the doctor, and if the cat accompanied her for the entire way and waited for her, she would take her home and name her.

By the end of her journey, the cat still by her side, not even wandering a bit. Adelia finally made it to the house in which the doctor lived and worked. Dr. Beeman did make many house calls, but for this particular conversation, a visit to the lighthouse would have been awkward at best.

"Now listen, girl." Adelia picked up the cat and smoothed her hand over the soft, black fur. "Wait for me, you hear? I won't be more than a few minutes."

She hoped she was right, and even more, prayed the cat would see her worthy of the wait. The feline stretched its back, seemingly standing tall, and offered up the slightest meow. It struck Adelia that the sound was almost regal and so was the cat. From the way she gracefully walked beside Adelia and seemed to understand much of what she was saying, there was a certain feel of royalty about the little girl. "You seem like a queen—or a princess, or wait—a duchess." With the way the cat held its head high, she could picture her as an aristocrat of sorts.

The cat rubbed her body along Adelia's hand, purring loudly. "Yes, you like that, do you?" Adelia clapped her hands together, a smile spreading over her face. "Duchess it is. I'll call you Duchess!" She had named the cat before seeing if she would actually wait; maybe it would work in her favor. "You wait right here for me, Duchess."

Knocking upon the door, Adelia breathed a sigh of relief at the sight of Mrs. Beeman.

"Hi, Mrs. Beeman. Adelia MacGregor here." She reached for the hand of the doctor's wife. Adelia had only met the doctor and his wife a few times and hoped she wasn't being perceived as too pushy by dropping by unannounced.

A wide smile spread over Mrs. Beeman's face, allowing

Adelia to relax a bit. She turned to follow the woman inside but then stopped to listen to Duchess cry out for her. She held up her finger, signaling she wouldn't be long.

"What brings you here so early in the morning?"

"I–um, this is a bit uncomfortable for me, and I hope I'm not being too presumptuous by asking if the doctor is available to speak with." Adelia felt heat spread across her cheeks. "If it's not too much trouble, that is."

"Who's that, Ellen?"

She craned her neck to see the doctor eating his breakfast at the dining room table, a book in hand.

"It's Adelia, the lighthouse keeper's wife from up on the bluffs."

Dr. Beeman wiped his hands on the cloth napkin in front of him and greeted Adelia with a jovial grin. "Yes, of course." He stood and waited for Adelia to respond.

"I'm sorry to intrude. It was very rude of me to barge in here while you're having your breakfast." Her face burned hotter. What had she been thinking? But then again, what other choice did she have?

"Nonsense, sit." He gestured toward an empty chair as Mrs. Beeman insisted upon pouring her some tea. As Adelia sipped at the tea, she had to admit it did help to steady her nerves a bit.

"Dr. Beeman, I came to you today because I'm worried, about my husband. I graciously ask that you please keep this meeting between us private."

Mrs. Beeman scurried off into another room, giving Adelia the privacy she needed to continue this conversation. This was her turning point; once she shared her concerns about Augustus with the doctor, she was admitting to someone besides herself and Devon that her marriage was in trouble and Augustus's problems were far worse.

"Of course. What can I do for you?"

She hesitated, pulling at her hair and fiddling with her pockets. "It's my husband, Augustus." She watched as a concerned look came across the doctor's face. He didn't speak, but his gaze urged her to continue on.

Feeling a bit more relaxed, she summoned up her courage. "This is rather awkward, so I'm just going to tell it as it is." She dared a glance at the doctor's face once more and then looked down. "Augustus has changed since our arrival here on Amity Island—a lot." She peeked at the doctor once more. "He's grown distant, bitter, angry, compulsive, and he's drinking, quite a bit. He won't even permit me to walk into town alone. He claims there's a thief wandering about. I had to sneak here to see you."

There, for whatever it was worth, the information was out in the open.

At first, Dr. Beeman just looked at her, then he cleared his throat. "Well, that's a lot to take in." He took a moment to compose himself. "As far as the thief goes, I have heard of this concern."

"From whom? I'm not even sure it's based on facts. Sometimes I feel as if he made the story up to keep me prisoner up there with him. I mean, what has actually been stolen?"

"I have heard of some items missing from several farms—some equipment, tools."

She shook her head; she didn't need to hear this, to have it cloud her judgment. "That's not the point. I fear he's going mad."

"I'm sorry, if I'm not mistaken, you're telling me that this behavior—it's all new?" He scratched his head.

"Well, yes. I mean, Augustus was known to have an occasional glass of gin, from time to time." Her mind went back to the boat ride over to the island. He had taken a drink of gin from a small bottle. She recalled thinking it was a bit out of character for him; she had rarely seen him partake in drinking alcohol, but how well did she actually know him before they married? It was a confusing thought. When they had first arrived, could he have been sneaking drinks here and there? When had his drinking shifted from social behavior to habit?

"It started gradually, beginning several weeks into our arrival here on the island. But it's getting worse, much worse with each passing day it seems. He's also becoming quite delusional. He stands firm on the belief that he's the first owner of the lighthouse and not only that, but that he built it himself." She paused, for her rapid breathing made it difficult to speak.

"But that's not true. Samuel Gordon and his crew built the lighthouse, and Thomas Fitzgerald and his wife, Emma, were the original keepers."

"Yes, I know that. The problem is that Augustus does not!" She stood and grabbed her skirts, nearly jumping out of her skin.

The doctor rose from his chair and took hold of her shoulders, shaking them slightly. "Calm down, Adelia, please." He released her before he began pacing the small spot in front of him. "Are you certain? I mean *really* certain?"

"I wish I wasn't; God, how I wish I wasn't! But it's true, and I'm growing fearful not only for Augustus, but for myself as well. I fear he's become dangerous."

She waited out the thick silence, which followed her bold admission. Why didn't he say something? *Anything?*

"What you're telling me here are some very harsh accusations." He averted his gaze from her as if uncomfortable with this information.

"I know—"

He pointed a long finger in the air, interrupting her. "Let me finish, please. I've met Augustus—several times, as a matter of fact. I had thought your husband was a good man, but it seems that he's in some trouble. I've heard of this before and have actually seen this type of thing and attempted to treat it, but to a much lesser degree, you see. Some of the symptoms are not uncommon for someone of your husband's position. It's got to be hard to be up there on the cliffs with such isolation. After a while . . . "

"It's treatable?" She jumped at the part where he mentioned some possibility of treatment. "Thank God. So there is hope."

"Mrs. MacGregor?" He gazed directly at her this time. "Sit down." Adelia's body tightened at the look on his face.

She counted to ten silently so she could catch her breath, and prayed for a positive outcome she knew wouldn't materialize. "Yes?" Her voice came out as a small squeak.

"I'm worried—for the both of you. I stated that what I had dealt with prior was to a much lesser degree. The science of behavior and of the mind is such new territory. This is out of my realm of experience. It sounds as if what you're saying is true, your husband might best be treated in an asylum."

Asylum? Wasn't that where deeply troubled individuals went when there was no other hope? And those patients lost all dignity—she doubted that most of them returned to the outside world, and those who did were often in worse condition than when they were admitted. The cruel, painful treatments that were exercised upon the patients—it hurt her head to even contemplate sending him to such a place.

Coming here may have been a mistake of gigantic proportions. "No, that's not what I had in mind at all. I think you've misunderstood."

"Wait. You claim Augustus is angry, delusional, and in an inebriated state most of the time? From the worry on your face when you arrived, I will even venture that you've left out some of the more disturbing actions on his part."

Her mind went to the endless hours of staring into space, the countless layers of paint on the lighthouse walls, counting the steps.

But an asylum?

She wouldn't wish that on her worst enemy. "I think I can help him. Please—just tell me where to begin."

The doctor barely contained his cryptic laughter. "Mrs. MacGregor? I don't think *I* can even help him. Would he agree to come speak with me? Is it safe for him to hold such a position of responsibility? We've had many a shipwreck in these waters, and I would hate to imagine—"

This *was* a mistake on her part. Now she couldn't even be sure their conversation would be kept confidential on the doctor's part. "Please, I beg you not to speak of this talk we've had. I had nowhere else to turn, and I promise you he takes his responsibilities as the keeper of the lighthouse seriously—almost to the point of compulsion—so there's no need to worry about the welfare of others."

"Except you." His eyes held true concern, and she felt herself relax just a bit.

"What advice did you give the other person you treated?"

He shook his head firmly. She wanted some chance, however slight it was, to get a piece of Augustus back.

"I don't like this at all." His face turned grim as his

features darkened. "I'm sorry, but I will need to make a necessary house call to see Augustus for myself."

"He can put on a different face at times, you may not see anything to arouse concern. If you come, Augustus will know I spoke to you, and he won't be happy with me." That was an understatement. She couldn't imagine her husband's reaction upon hearing of her betrayal—for that's what he would consider this to be: a betrayal of the worst kind.

"Give me a few days, Dr. Beeman, that's all I ask." She didn't know what a few days would buy her but time. At this point, it was all she had.

"I should run up there right now, Adelia. I really should." She held her breath as she saw his eyes soften just a bit. "But I will give you a few days, and then I'm coming to see for myself."

All she could do was thank him and admonish herself for coming here. She had only made matters worse. "In the meantime, Doctor, is there anything at all you could suggest?"

"Do you still love him, Adelia?"

She hesitated and finally answered the question she refused to ask herself earlier. Did she love him? Yes, as a person with whom she had shared some wonderful earlier memories with. If by some miracle he came out of this for the best, she would stand by his side and be true to him.

Was she *in love* with him?

Devon's face flashed before her, his full hair, the warmth of his eyes when he gazed at her . . . she knew Devon was the one whom she would cry out for in the middle of the night, but she also knew she would deny her heart until the bitter end.

"Yes." She omitted the complications of her heart and

pulled her head up to face the doctor. "Yes, I do." She waited for him to question her own sanity but knew that it was very rare for a woman to leave her husband, regardless of the reason. She wasn't surprised that he didn't flinch.

"Talk to him, keep talking, and remind him of better times. Do little things for him that will show him you care. In other words, be your most cheerful, upbeat self. Give him plenty of hearty meals and one other thing." The doctor's eyes gleamed and he suddenly looked like a jolly, mischievous comrade.

"What?"

"The alcohol he's been drinking could be exacerbating his symptoms. Is there any chance you can dilute his drink with water?"

"Watering down his gin?" She supposed she could, but if he found out, he would be very angry. She could try. She could.

"I don't think it will be the ultimate answer, but it can only help. I fear we both know the outcome of this predicament, but I will give you a couple of days, as I promised. If he's as far gone as you claim, it will be your chance to say goodbye."

The finality of his statement hurt her. It was too sad to contemplate. "Are you sure this is the best way?" She grabbed hold of the doctor's collar and then realized her misstep. He merely glanced at her and straightened his shirt.

"Yes, I am. And Adelia?" He reached for her hands, making direct eye contact. "It might be time to consider this could be part of your own boredom manifesting—for that could easily happen to you as well." Her breath hitched, and words escaped her as the doctor rambled on. "If all seems well when I visit, then I won't worry too much about *him.*"

He eyed her cautiously. He couldn't possibly think *she*

was the one who was going mad, could he? Before Adelia had a chance to register anger at his statement, the doctor changed course.

"On the other hand, if I confront him, and he goes into a rage, as I suspect someone in that state could possibly do, then I will recommend a replacement for him at the lighthouse and a place for Augustus to seek treatment."

An asylum. This was awful, but so was her existence with Augustus on the bluffs. Where did any of this leave her? She knew the only place she could return to heal after all this heartbreak would be home. There would be no place left for her here on the island if Augustus were to be taken from her. Devon would be long gone, too.

Devon.

As much as she wished she could include him in her visions of the future, she knew that for now, at least, although their hearts were tied, it wasn't meant to be. Maybe in another lifetime they would meet before either had committed to another.

She would go home.

Home to her family, friends, her mother. She envisioned herself already wrapped in her mother's warm arms—the scent of sugar and flour, all the warm, pleasant smells of her childhood. She conjured up her mother's loving face and attempted to steady her shaking hands by placing them in her pockets.

"I'm giving you two days—three, at the most, before I come calling." His ominous words sounded as if they came from a great distance, and she recalled feeling as if she were outside of herself for the briefest of moments.

"Did you hear me? Adelia, are you okay?" The doctor held his hand on her shoulder. "You did the right thing by coming here. If what you say is true, it was the only course of action."

She nodded, quietly thanking him as if she were in a trance. Neither spoke another word as he walked her toward the door. She wasn't sure, but she could have sworn she glimpsed a slight movement, perhaps a shadow from around the corner? Had Mrs. Beeman overheard their conversation? If so, what did it even matter anymore? In a few days time, her life as she knew it would be upended, and all of the residents of this island would speculate about what had become of the lighthouse keeper and his wife. The doctor closed the door softly behind her, leaving Adelia alone with her thoughts.

Adelia remained on the porch of the doctor's house, leaning against the door as she collected herself. Suddenly, she remembered the cat.

Where was Duchess? Amongst all of the heartbreaking events that had come tumbling at her as of late, the absence of the cat topped it all off. Adelia crumbled to the ground, not caring if her dress got dirty, not caring if people strolling by saw her. She was alone. Even Duchess had left her.

But then, she heard a faint sound, and strained her ears to make sure she wasn't imagining things. Adelia could have burst with delight as a black bundle of fur came bounding at her from down a nearby hill, voicing her own joy with an abundance of meows. When Duchess finally reached her, she held on, clinging to the cat like a lifeline.

CHAPTER SEVENTEEN

2017

It was too much.

Way too much.

"What happened? What did you feel back there?" Clooney had thanked Jane and then carefully ushered Hope to the car.

How could she explain? Even she had a tough time trying to understand why Jane's words had affected her so strongly. "I don't know exactly, I'm still trying to process everything."

"What do you mean? Hope, tell me something."

"I said I don't know!" She spat out the words and covered her head in her hands. A growing headache stole whatever small amount of patience Hope had right now.

The wife of the lighthouse keeper had kept a secret lover? Who killed her, tossed her down the stairs to her death? No–her gut told her that there was something off here. Misinformation? Maybe, but also there was more.

Something on the precipice of her mind, so close, but then it was gone again.

Clooney whistled and sat back against the car seat. His hands gripped the steering wheel tightly. The uncomfortable silence didn't help to lessen the pounding in her head. This time she wasn't even in the mood to offer up an apology to him. It irked her how he pressed her at times. Space—before this relationship with Clooney, she pretty much had all of the space she could ever need. All the nuances that made up her new relationship with Clooney were exhausting at times.

"I guess you want to go home?" Clooney started the ignition, his eyes on the road ahead. She merely nodded.

Forget about a trip to the library and town clerk's office; their one stop had been about all she could handle. Clooney had pressed her for answers, but the problem still lay in the fact that it was more of a feeling than anything else. Finding out that a man and a woman had been pushed down the stairs would upset anyone, but considering that she had front row seats to the event on a regular basis, it hit her harder. Still, why had she been so floored to find that it was the woman's lover that had pushed both Augustus and Adelia down those steps?

That was the burning question.

The answer was close, almost right there within her reach once more, but then it dissolved right before her.

Clooney made the short trip back to Hope's, and walked her into the house. He hesitated at the door, but she took his hand and guided him inside. Now she felt remorse at being short with him. She also felt the stress of how she had been treated differently than him by Jane at the historical society. Now, each and every face that had ever stared *at* her, *through* her, consumed her mind.

"I'm sorry."

He shook his head, a line of irritation creasing his face. "Stop saying that."

"But I am. Clooney?" Her eyes searched his face for answers to a question she knew he couldn't answer.

"What, Hope?"

"What is it about me that others find so . . . disturbing?" For lack of a better word, it was all she could come up with.

"Disturbing? Honey, what are you talking about?" But she saw his face turn down and then the look in his eye, as if he was trying too hard to act as if he had no idea what she meant.

"You see it, you'd be blind not to. The way people look at me, *through* me, as if I don't exist. They hate me."

"Stop it, Hope, just stop. Nobody hates you. They don't know you is all, not the way I do."

"I try. I'm shy, but dammit, I go out of my comfort zone to try to talk to people, try to make friends." Her breath hitched as she fought back tears.

"You have Tracy and you have me. If they knew you like we know you—"

"Stop." She held a hand up to silence him. "They don't, but you're right. You and Tracy mean more to me than a thousand useless faces." She should be counting her blessings to have found two such wonderful people to call friends and instead she was just feeling sorry for herself.

He stood before her and clasped onto her hands. "Hope? Will you do something for me?"

"Of course." She rubbed at her eyes.

"Will you get some help, please? Talk to someone?"

Therapy? "Clooney, I'm fine." She knew her lame attempt at normalcy was a joke, but she couldn't think about therapy right now.

"I just got overwhelmed back there. I felt a rush of emotions—fear, anger, curiosity. It all came at me at once, even had me wondering about us."

"Us? What about us?"

"Clooney, you know I love you, but sometimes my feelings for you scare the hell out of me. I feel so strongly about you—maybe *too* strongly."

He stepped back. "I don't understand."

She was probably scaring the crap out of him, but she didn't care right now. She had to get this off her chest. "I want you here."

"Okay. I love being here with you."

"Please, Clooney, for the love of God, let me finish a complete thought." He didn't respond, but his eyes turned down for a moment. "I know you like being here, but I get scared when you leave—like I'm never going to see you again."

He waited a beat. "Can I talk now?"

"Yes, of course."

"I'm not leaving you. Yes, Hope, I may have to go to work, go home, see my friends, but I'm not leaving this. I'm not leaving *us*."

She appreciated his honesty and trusted that he meant what he said—right now. "Thank you, and I believe that you mean what you say, but things change. People change."

His voice rose, attempting to bring the point home. "Hope, this is all coming from one place, your insecurity about leaving your house. Get the help you need for it, and everything else will follow. If you get out and lead your own life, you won't be obsessing over every detail about things that can go wrong when I'm out of your sight."

He was making her sound pathetic, but he did have a point. She might consider talking to someone after they found some answers. "I would consider it. I've thought of going to see someone before. Until now, I never had much reason to even want to head into town."

Now, there was Clooney. Now, she needed to find answers, and going into town was the best way, but it still didn't mean she had the strength to change that right now.

"After all this, Clooney, after we figure out what these visions mean, I'll think about it."

"It could help if you go now. These visions could have something to do with your anxiety."

"Oh, I see. So it's all in my head." She cursed under her breath, knowing she wasn't being fair to him.

"Hope, I'm trying so hard to show you that I'm here for you, that you can't get rid of me. I don't get you. At times it's almost like you want to push me away."

Before he does it first.

She felt tears rising and turned away from him.

"Hope?" He placed his hand on her shoulder.

"I'm sorry, you're right."

He chuckled lightly. "Didn't I just ask you not to say that?"

She laughed, and it eased some of the tension away. "Old habits."

"You'll think about talking to someone?"

"Soon." It was the best she could offer. She made her way to the cabinet and took out some tea bags. She needed to chill out. "Would you like a cup?"

"Sure." He helped her by grabbing a spoon and some milk out of the fridge. "So what's the plan for the short-term?"

Her mind considered their next course of action as she wondered why all of this came down to her.

"Why is this woman haunting *me*?" She already knew the most likely answer to the quandary, but still. Had the other occupants of the lighthouse encountered the same experiences? Tracy hadn't.

"Technically, I don't think she's haunting you."

She spun to face him, ready to pounce, but then thought back to their recent conversation. "Then what would you call it?" she asked as calmly as she possibly could.

He continued, "Have you heard anything unusual, besides the visions? Has anything been moved around? Have you seen any apparitions?"

Huh. "Well, no."

"So you're not being haunted. You're just having dreams."

Oh, if only his words were that simple. Did he not grasp the significance of those visions?

"Dreams?" she scoffed, this time unable to keep her irritation from surfacing. "Just dreams, you say? Clooney, these are most definitely not *just dreams*. They haunt me during the night, they sneak up on me and stalk me by day." She huffed and pouted a moment. Sipping at her tea, she eyed him from over the rim of her mug.

Then she had a thought. "Say, I wonder if we could get in touch with some of the previous tenants of the property, besides Tracy, that is."

"I guess it couldn't hurt."

"Can you look into that for me? I'm going to make a few phone calls. I figured I'd call the Chamber of Commerce. I don't think it's a good idea for me to go into town again so soon."

His look said it all, but she knew he wouldn't argue

with her right now. "I was also thinking that I wish I knew more about your roots here. Is there any way you could ask someone in your family?"

"I suppose I could try. Why is that important?"

"Maybe someone would remember hearing something more about that story. You never know what lies in people's attics. Your parents might know something." She knew from a previous conversation that his parents lived in New Jersey, down by the shore.

"I doubt it, but I'll ask."

"When was the last time they cleaned out their attic?"

"They moved down to the shore after my dad retired a few years ago, so I'm sure they cleaned some stuff out, and they probably remember what they did choose to keep."

It was a stretch to think that items or artifacts from his great-great-grandparents and beyond would still exist, but it was possible.

"Okay, let's get started. Let me know what you find out." She glanced at the clock on the kitchen wall. "Say we meet back here in a few hours?"

"Hope, I have to work tonight. I'll head to the clerk's office and give you a call after, okay?"

"Sure." She felt a sudden need to keep him here where she could see him, know that he wouldn't leave her. "Are you coming back tonight after work?"

"Yes, but I think you and Tracy should make up, so I'll only stay for a bit and then give you guys some space."

"Oh." But she had assumed after the night they had shared that he would consider staying over again. *Reel it in.*

"It'll be fine. Remember, I'm here and I'm not going anywhere." He kissed her gently, and she enjoyed the distraction of the feel of his mouth, the rising passion between them.

"Do we have time for a break before we both get to work?" His eyes sparkled as he smoothed her hair from her face.

"I think we could manage that." She grabbed his head and pulled it down so that she could kiss him once more. They had plenty of time to work; right now all she wanted to do was escape her troubles and lose herself in him.

CHAPTER EIGHTEEN
2017

Tracy gave off a distant vibe as she took charge and handled the tourists. Hope, in a quiet mood, stood back and imagined what it would be like when Tracy was gone for good. Would Tracy's replacement live with her at the house? Would it be a person with a family? How would that work? Nobody could ever replace her friend, and here she had gone and screwed everything up. It seemed as if the visitors arrived in an endless stream throughout the day, giving Hope little opportunity to have a word with Tracy in private.

When the last visitor of the day had departed, Hope worked up her courage and approached Tracy. "Trace? Do you have a second?"

"I guess."

"Listen, I'm sorry. The way I acted was inexcusable."

"Don't apologize, Hope. Just think about what I said about getting some help."

"I am, and I've decided that I will talk to someone."

Tracy's brows rose. "You will?"

"Yes, Clooney and I were just talking about it. He asked me to as well."

"Well . . . that's good."

"Just as soon as I figure out the mystery behind these visions."

Tracy blew out a breath. "I really think—"

"I know, but please. Let me do this my way. Right now, I have to focus all of my energy on figuring this out. Once I do, I'll make an appointment. Promise."

"Oh, Hope. I do love you, but you drive me crazy sometimes. I mean, I worry about you so much, especially with me moving away."

"Don't even get started on that, Trace. Just concentrate on planning the best wedding ever, and I will be fine. As much as you think Clooney has something to do with the regression of my behavior, as you call it, he doesn't. Clooney is just as worried about me as you are, if that makes you feel any better."

"It doesn't make me feel better. Oh, fine, it's good that he cares about you. I just don't want him to hurt you. Very few people *get* you, Hope."

She reached for Tracy's hand and squeezed it gently. "He does. Rest assured, he does. I want you to come home, tonight, please."

Tracy studied Hope's face and caved. "Sure. I missed you, you little brat." Tracy swatted her arm and laughed.

"Good, I missed you, too." She smiled, and added, "You little brat."

Hope and Tracy worked on closing things up at the lighthouse so that they could lock up for the day. Clooney would be coming over after his shift for a bit, and Hope had promised to wait for him so that they could have dinner together. She needed to get home to start on the meal.

"I'm making some pasta and chicken tonight for me and Clooney if you feel like joining us."

She waited out the pause, hoping that Tracy would consider giving Clooney another chance. Hope knew that once she spent some more time with him, she would feel better about everything.

"I'd like that."

Hope beamed. "Great. You can invite Tommy, too, if you want."

"He's working later, but thanks."

Hope was glad to have her friend back, and now that their dispute was settled, her mind drifted back to her immediate problem. She wondered why she had never questioned Tracy about the previous lighthouse keepers before.

"Do you know much about the other lighthouse keepers who came before us?"

"Well, there was Adam Kincaid and his family just before we arrived, and then, I think it was a single man. I don't recall much more. Why?"

"I just got to thinking, why am I the one receiving these visions instead of you?"

Tracy waited a moment before responding. "I'm sorry to say this, but I think it might tie into your phobias and anxiety, Hope."

Great. Another person telling her it was all in her head.

"That's why I think it might be a good idea to—"

She held her hand in the air, cutting Tracy off. "Stop, just stop, it is not stemming from my anxiety, trust me on that one."

"Well, then, I have no answer for you."

"Clooney's helping me out. He's looking into that angle, talking to previous workers, seeing if anyone else felt something strange here."

"Hope, I wish I had answers for you about this. Doesn't it tell you something that I haven't been hit with these dreams and visions?"

"Not really. For some reason, this woman has chosen me to help her sort out this mess. *Me,* and I'm not going to disappoint her."

Dinner couldn't have gone better. Hope sat back and studied her two most favorite people in this world. She got to thinking that the only thing that could have made the evening better was if her mother was here.

She should have invited her mother. Hope hadn't seen her in such a long time, and she knew that mother would have made the trip if she had asked.

Your mother is dead.

"Hope? Are you okay?" Clooney stopped talking to Tracy and centered his gaze on Hope.

A wash of heat, followed by a rush of cold, swept through her body, leaving her confused and disoriented. "What?"

"Are you okay?" This time it was Tracy, who stood and made her way over to Hope's side.

"Yes, yes. I'm fine." Her hand went into her pocket and she rubbed her fingers back and forth against the length of the stone.

How had she forgotten again that her mother was dead?

Her friends were right to worry for her. Her mother had been her most consistent source of comfort, and she missed her so much. With all of this ghost business, it was no wonder she was reaching out for the solace of her mom.

"You're pale; drink this." Clooney handed her a glass of water. She reached for it as her hand trembled.

She needed to speed things up with the investigation. Her stress was creeping through in so many ways, and she figured it was bound to become worse if she didn't get answers soon.

And there was something else that still kept spiraling around in her head, making her stress skyrocket. It was that business of the lover again. Why? She was getting too close, the mystery of the lighthouse keeper's wife and her lover was beckoning her to discover the truth behind the rumors and stories.

It was all-consuming.

Placing her head in her hands, Hope sighed deeply. She needed to focus her thoughts elsewhere for the time-being as answers weren't forthcoming.

"Did you find out anything today?" She directed her question at Clooney.

"Besides the family that was here before you guys, I found the name of a man. Peter Frond. He was the keeper for a long time. A very long time—over thirty years. I made some calls and was able to contact one of his children. Seems that Peter is in a nursing home and suffers from Alzheimer's."

"Well, that's too bad. I doubt Peter would be much help to us. And the family right before we got here?"

"Found them, too. I spoke with Adam Kincaid himself. He claimed that despite some creaks here and there and the rumor of an old ghost story, nothing was amiss."

"Every old building with history seems to have a ghost

story. That's why I never gave much thought to the stories about this place—until now, that is," Tracy offered.

'Where is Peter now? Is the nursing home on the island?" Hope wondered if it would be worth a visit.

"No such luck. The home is over on the mainland in Pine Island. I suppose I could make the trip . . ." He glanced over at Hope, and she knew what he was thinking. There was no way she would make the ferry trip; it was tough enough going down the road lately.

"If you want, but I'm busy here." Her comment caused Clooney and Tracy to lock eyes. "I don't even know if it makes sense to go."

"It couldn't hurt." Clooney sipped at his glass of wine. The thought of Clooney making a trip off this island suddenly didn't sit well with her.

"No. No, I'd rather you stay here with me. I need all the help I can get."

Another look passed between her friends. Clooney cleared his throat and continued on. "So I also called my parents, and they said they don't know much about my own family's history on the island here, other than the fact that many of my relatives and ancestors liked to vacation here. Oh yes, and I found that my great-great-grandfather definitely lived here for a short period of time."

"How did you find that out?"

"I asked my uncle. My uncle Mike is a history buff. My dad told me to give him a call. Seems Mike is into all those ancestry websites where you can trace your roots. Anyway, he claims our roots go way back here, back to the 1800s." He paused, a proud grin settling on his face.

"That is pretty cool," Tracy added. "What was your great-great-grandfather's name?"

Hope felt herself distance from them before he spoke the name. The quality of the air actually shifted around her; she knew they felt it too. She watched Tracy shiver and wrap her arms across her chest. Almost as if from a cold, dark tunnel, she listened as Clooney was seconds away from saying the name of his great-great-grandfather.

Now, a vivid slideshow of images hit her from all angles– a timeline of events forming, settling all around her, suffocating her, until she couldn't stand it– the last pieces of the puzzle shifted together and Hope almost wanted to stop him, because once Clooney spoke those words, once they came out of his mouth, everything would change.

"Devon. Devon Bane."

CHAPTER NINETEEN

1876

SHE MADE THE walk back to the lighthouse, clutching Duchess in her arms and, at times, letting her walk beside her up the winding dirt road. She could follow the doctor's orders and be nice to Augustus, extra kind, even. She would prepare his favorite dinner, the stew he loved so much. As far as watering down the gin, she would look through the cabinets where his supply was kept and dump out just enough that he wouldn't suspect anything.

"Come on, baby," Adelia whispered to Duchess as they approached the lighthouse. "This is it. This is your new home."

Was it her imagination or did the cat's heart thump a little faster, louder? Or was it her own pulse quickening at the sight of the home? "It'll be okay. You and I will be in this together."

She squinted her eyes and scanned the top of the tower.

She didn't see Augustus up there, but he was probably still immersed in his work. If all went as she hoped, he would still be painting those walls like a maniac, and he wouldn't have missed her.

"Home sweet home, Duchess." She opened the door and placed the black cat inside the main entrance. Duchess appeared intent to stick by her side and not wander off. Adelia made her way to the kitchen, attempting to walk as quietly as possible. Her chest heaved a sigh of relief as she walked into the empty room.

The first thing she did was to give the cat a saucer of milk, then she went to gather some water and prepare the tea. Augustus might come down at any moment, and she wished to make everything appear as normal as possible. She recalled what the doctor had advised and made an extra cup for Augustus. While waiting for the water to warm on the wood stove, she walked back out to the entrance of the lighthouse and peeked up the stairs.

"Augustus?" No response.

Of course not.

But that meant for now, the coast was clear. Tying on an apron, she took the opportunity to hustle back to the kitchen and find the jugs in which Augustus kept his gin. One container at a time, with Duchess at her feet like a trusty companion, Adelia carefully emptied about a third of the liquid in each jug into a large basin and refilled them with water. She would dump the gin outside, where she normally disposed of the dirty water, in the brush near the top of the cliff.

She had better hurry, for she could only imagine her husband's reaction if he caught her red-handed, a bucket of gin in hand. "Come on, girl," she called out to Duchess.

All would appear ordinary if Augustus spotted her outside. He wouldn't give it a second thought. With shaking hands, Adelia dumped the gin into the bushes and said a silent prayer that she was doing the right thing. He couldn't possibly detect that she had tampered with his drink—at least she hoped not.

"There." She wiped her hands on her small apron. Next, she would bring Augustus a cup of tea.

"Come on, Duchess." She turned toward the cat, but found her missing. "Duchess, Duchess!" Oh, where could that cat have taken off to? She cried out again, her eyes scanning the vast property. A streak of black flashed and then disappeared under the latticework on the bottom of the lighthouse.

"Oh no you don't. You're going to find nothing but trouble under there." She scurried toward the lighthouse, quickening her step. God only knew what was under there— dirt, animals. "Duchess!"

Duchess didn't materialize, so Adelia did the only thing she could think to do. With a sigh, she got down on her hands and knees and peeked through the lattice. She saw the glow of the cat's eyes and cried out again. Duchess meowed but didn't cooperate. "You're not going to make this easy for me, are you?" Another meow.

"Come on, Duchess. I'm not going in there for you." She pried open the woodwork a bit wider around the spot where the cat must have entered.

"That's strange." Augustus didn't let anything go when it came to the upkeep of this building. The wood was loose enough to pull out a large section—big enough to fit through.

"I'm only coming this far, Duchess. You'll be much happier staying inside with me." But she figured Duchess had wandered around the outdoors all of her young life until she had found her. The cat barely knew anything else.

"Fine. Come and go as you wish. I give up." She scooted backwards, and that's when her eye caught hold of something in the far corner. Was that a flail? Yes, it was. The farming tool which was used to thresh grains sat there, glaringly obvious. Next to it was a scythe. She knew for a fact that Augustus did not own either. He was not on this island to farm or fish like most—he was the lighthouse keeper. Period.

Her heart must have stopped beating for a moment; she could scarcely breathe. "Oh my God," she whispered, her hands trembling as she covered her mouth—she couldn't scream. She could not scream. She looked around further, and sure enough, several other tools lay in piles close to the original find.

What would happen if he found her under here, discovering his darkest secrets? She scrambled back, crying out in pain as she hit her lower back on a rock. That darn cat just stared at her, still refusing to move.

She replaced the lattice as best she could with her hands still quivering. "Calm down," she muttered to herself. "There has to be some kind of explanation." She shoved her hands forcefully into her pockets to still the shaking and knew she was lying to herself.

There were no coincidences when it came to her life here with Augustus. There was only one possibility; her mind just needed to accept it as fact.

Augustus had been the thief all along.

All of this, just to keep her from wandering off the property? Instilling seeds of fear and doubt to keep her his prisoner? What she had suspected had now become the cold, hard truth.

But for what purpose?
And to what end?

"GET A HOLD of yourself," she mumbled like one of the patients in the feared asylums she hated to think of. "Get it together before he suspects that I'm on to him." She spoke in whispers, somehow needing to speak the words aloud to allow reality to settle in.

"Meow."

She jumped back, hurtling against the kitchen countertop. "Duchess!" Clutching at her chest, she nearly scolded the cat for sneaking up on her, but instead, she scooped her up in her arms, seeking comfort from the only living thing in this lighthouse that could provide it.

"What am I going to do, girl? What am I going to do?" She sobbed into the warm body of her companion.

"What's going on here?"

Adelia gasped aloud, squeezing the cat tight to her pounding chest. There was no disguising the tears in her eyes; she didn't even attempt to hide them at this point.

"Augustus."

"Why are you crying, and what is that *thing?*"

He curled up his lip in disgust at Duchess. The cat squirmed and hissed as he drew closer.

At least she's a good judge of character.

"This is Duchess. She's mine, ours."

"I don't want some stray, feral cat inside this house. Put it outside. It looks like it's starving half to death, and it just threatened me."

"She hissed at you because you scared her. She's the farthest thing from wild, Augustus. You told me to get a cat—to get rid of the mice, remember?" She would not allow Augustus to send Duchess back out onto the streets.

"Well, I don't remember saying that but, fine, we do have to keep the mice out. Just keep it out of my way."

She could have wept with relief. He had even forgotten to ask why she had been crying. She wiped her eyes and swallowed.

She spotted the mugs on the counter and remembered the water warming on the woodstove. Despite the alarming turn of events, she had to follow through with her original plan of killing him with kindness.

"Thanks, Augustus. I prepared some tea for you. Give me one minute." He eyed her warily, and she wondered when she had last surprised him with a gesture such as tea, just because.

"Thank you, Adelia."

As she turned from grabbing the water, she spied him rifling through the pantry. "A little gin in tea never hurt anyone, now did it?" He raised a jug and grinned at her.

Please, please, please.

She prayed he didn't taste the difference. She watched as he grabbed the mug from her and poured some gin in. Pausing to taste his tea, he frowned. "Not quite right, yet." He poured a bit more, tasted it, and then hurried back to the tower.

She was relieved but knew she wasn't out of the woods yet. It would have been difficult to determine if the gin had been watered down within a cup of tea, she supposed. Let's see what happened when he drank it straight.

She had dinner to prepare for, and mentally, she needed

to get in the right frame of mind to say her final farewell to Devon this evening. As she cleaned up the counter and washed her mug, her mind wandered back to Devon, and she wondered if it would always be this way. What would it be like to grow old with Augustus, or possibly alone, with her heart rooted to Devon? Would she look back as an older woman, gray hair and wrinkles staining her face, with her heart full of regret and lost chances?

Before she got too caught up in her own head, Adelia forced a smile and straightened her back. There was still a bit of warm water left, and she wondered if Augustus might want some more tea. If she was going to play this out, she would have to give it one hundred percent.

"Augustus?" She didn't know why she even bothered to call out his name. He probably stood smugly, enjoying the fact that she had to climb each step to speak with him.

By the time she got to almost the last step, she saw him. Huffing, she figured the tea was most likely cold by now. "Augustus?" Still, no answer as he swept a large paintbrush on the walls near the top of the tower.

Back and forth.

Back and forth.

A thin sheen of sweat covered his face and pooled on top of his upper lip. She didn't think the paint could look any better than it already did.

"Sweetheart, do you want some more tea?"

"Augustus? Did you hear me?"

Silence. And more swiping of the paintbrush.

Swish. Swish. Swish.

"Augustus? Here, I brought some more tea for you." She held on to the mug, bringing it closer, until it was practically under his nose.

"What are you doing here?" He snapped the words, stiffening his back at seeing her.

A wild, unleashed look came over his face, his eyes alight with fury. Adelia shrank back, nearly dropping the mug. So this was the response she got for trying to be nice.

"I'm just seeing if you'd like some more tea. *Sweetheart.*" This was killing her, acting her sweetest to him with little in return.

"Tea?"

Her eyes widened, taking in his baffled expression. "Yes, tea."

As if a switch went off, his eyes almost seemed to glaze over and a softer, kinder look came over his features. "Tea. Yes, darling. That would be nice." He glanced at the empty mug on the floor as she bent down to reach for it. She even leaned over and kissed him full on the mouth for good measure. Although the kiss lasted a few seconds, it lacked desire and passion. Gone was the spunky, playful spark that used to light up his eyes.

Adelia handed him the fresh cup of tea and turned to go back down the stairs.

"Darling?"

"Yes, what is it?" But she knew. Gin. He wanted his gin. She walked up a few more steps to the tower and reached for the jug on the floor.

Empty.

"It's empty, dear." She hoped he would just drink the damn tea and forget the gin for once.

"Would you be a darling and grab me another jug? I'll need more anyway."

What she wanted to say was *get your own damn jug and stick it up your behind.* "Of course." Her counterfeit smile hurt, but she kept it in place until he was out of sight.

Adelia sighed and did her best to hurry down the stairs. The thought of traveling back up and then down these steps once more soured her mood. She had lots to do and getting Augustus his gin would have to be the last attempt at sugaring him up until dinnertime. When he tasted his gin separate from the tea later, she would find out if she had fooled him.

She spotted Duchess lingering around the bottom of the staircase, weaving her body around the railing. The cat glanced up and meowed.

"What's the matter, baby?"

Again, she voiced her opinion, but this time it was more of a howl that erupted from the cat.

"What?" Adelia looked up the staircase. "You don't want to go up there?" She chuckled harshly. Leaning over, she whispered in the cat's ear. "Can't say I blame you." The comment earned a deep purr.

She made her way to kitchen and grabbed the jug from the cupboard. She almost wished she hadn't watered down the gin yet. She wanted him passed out cold for when she visited with Devon later. Then again, Augustus had been up extra early that morning, and his glass had been right beside him.

It should be fine.

Before she returned upstairs, she grabbed the items she would need to prepare dinner and placed them on the counter.

Back up the stairs. Duchess lingered at the bottom, swirling and howling incessantly. Adelia shook her head. *Strange cat.*

Gasping for breath, she ascended the stairs until she

reached the top once more. It looked like he had finished painting for the day. Instead of painting, he now took his usual stance at the window of the tower, staring.

Just staring.

"Here you go." She took the mug of tea from the spot on the floor next to him. He didn't flinch, just kept his eyes glued to what lay beyond the window. Adelia quickly poured some gin into the mug and stood with the cup of tea in hand, waiting for him to take it, waiting for him to show some sign that he knew she was standing there. "Augustus."

When he turned to face her, it was done slowly and deliberately. "Thank you." He accepted the mug from her and then leaned over to place the tea on the floor. "I'm not in the mood for tea anymore."

"Oh." Wonderful. She just loved running up and down these stairs for no reason.

"Did you not notice all of the painting I've done today?"

How could she not? "Yes. Yes, of course. "

"And?" He leaned forward until she could smell his rancid gin breath.

"And it looks good."

"Good?" He chuckled bitterly. A chill coursed through her, and she knew where his mood was headed. "Good, you say?"

"Very good. It looks wonderful."

"Don't you patronize me, Adelia. I work hard, day and night, and all you can say is that it looks *good*?"

She backed away a few feet, hoping he would go back to staring out the window. She knew what he wanted to hear. This was yet another quirk he added to his list of already obnoxious behaviors. "Thank you, Augustus. Thank you so much for making our home clean and beautiful." She bit down on her lip, praying that would be enough to calm him down.

He swore, his head shaking back and forth until it stilled. When his gaze bore down on her again, he spoke. "You're welcome. I just hope you appreciate, I mean *truly* appreciate, all I do for you, for our home. I built this home . . ."

She couldn't stand listening to this– One. More. Time.

As he spoke, she attempted to block out his words with thoughts—good thoughts, mostly of her family. "And I thank you so much for that, Augustus." She had to play the game, for the other option of telling him how she truly felt looked dangerous from where she stood.

"Now bring me up something to eat." He gazed down at the jug of gin she had brought him. "Please."

The stew wasn't close to being ready. It was early, hours before suppertime. "I'll bring you a snack. Dinner isn't ready yet, but I'm preparing your favorite stew tonight. What would you like to hold you over?"

"Figure it out, and hurry up about it. I have more work to do, and I'd like to enjoy my dinner at a decent hour."

"Yes." She cursed him over and over with each countless step as she descended down to where Duchess sat, waiting for her.

As she prepared his snack, she wondered if she was better off just ignoring Augustus. It seemed the kinder she treated him, the more he took advantage of her.

His snack consisted of slices of apples, some grapes, and cheese. She munched on some of the fruit that was left on the counter and offered the cat a small piece of the cheese.

Step by step, she traveled the stairs again, finding herself even more winded than before. "Here you go." She panted the words.

"What is this?"

"It's the snack you asked for, you said you were hungry."

He spat on the floor next to her feet. "I say I'm hungry, and you bring me rabbit food? Take it back. I'm not hungry anymore."

Words escaped her, for she feared what would come flying out of her mouth at this moment.

That did it. Forget about playing nice, Dr. Beeman. Right now, she wished the good doctor would come along and take Augustus to the dreaded asylum. With shaking hands, she fought back the words she so desperately wanted to shriek. Augustus turned his back on her and poured some gin from the jug into his glass.

For a second, she forgot all about watering down his gin. She forgot about everything except the yearning of her very soul. She cried inside for the child she had once been. Was this what she would want for her own child someday? To suffer like this? Such a cruel fate she had been handed.

Then it hit her. Maybe, just maybe, that premonition of her falling was what would happen if she *stayed*. Was she meant to leave here before that final act could be played out? Is that why she and Devon had crossed paths? Confusion clouded out all rational thoughts—except one.

She wanted better.

She deserved so much more.

At that moment, she had nearly forgotten that Augustus stood before her; her problem front and center.

Almost.

She should have known the second she saw him, should have backed away when she had the chance. Instead, she stood, unable to move as the glass of gin flew at her, landing inches from her feet. Shards of glass exploded in every direction, one puncturing her face, mere millimeters from her eye. She wailed, pulling out the tiny sliver of glass.

Piece upon piece of the broken glass lay at her feet and down, through the tiny holes in the honeycomb patterned floor.

Don't cry. Do not let him see your fear.

"What in bloody hell did you do to my gin?" he bellowed. His rage increased with each impending step.

"I have no idea what you're talking about!" She stood firm, but then backed toward the edge of the stairs as his sweaty face turned a sick, crimson shade.

She backed up, knowing she was drawing closer to the top of the stairs. She needed to make a break for it, had to turn and run at just the precise moment.

"This gin tastes like crap! Crap, crap, crap!"

Now.

She made a break for the stairs and nearly stumbled as she took in the jagged pieces of broken glass on the steps leading down. Was he following her? She didn't dare look back.

In the distance she could hear his screaming, but it was becoming more muffled with her descent. She followed the sound of Duchess's meowing, startled to see that the cat had, indeed, started its path up the stairs toward her.

"Come." She grabbed Duchess, and together they made it to the bottom of the steps. She collapsed on the floor.

Seemed like the doctor's advice backfired. She was sure Dr. Beeman had nothing but good intentions, but unfortunately, Augustus was too far gone for this. Now she wished that she hadn't told the doctor to give her a few days. Maybe she would make a trip into town tomorrow morning and tell the doctor she had changed her mind.

If she continued staying here, only one of them would survive. It was her or him—of that she was sure. She wouldn't watch as Augustus drank himself into oblivion and tried to take her down with him.

Everything suddenly became clear, and she was never more certain of what she needed to do. She counted the minutes until she would meet Devon on top of the bluffs.

CHAPTER TWENTY
1876

She needed to eat, needed her strength. Otherwise, she probably wouldn't have bothered to cook tonight. She hadn't heard a word from Augustus since his outburst a couple of hours ago. Since everything for the stew was already set to go, she had prepared the meal, now hating that is was his favorite.

She lifted a finger to touch the cut beneath her eye. At first, she had cried after Augustus had thrown the glass at her, curled up in a ball with Duchess lying by her side. Once she had finished feeling sorry for herself, anger replaced sadness.

Now? Now she felt a hardened indifference. She would make dinner, go through the motions of being his wife until she could escape. After this was all over, she would look back and feel nothing put pity for the man she had married. Whether this sickness was inherited from relatives or whether it stemmed from boredom up here on the bluffs, drinking too much, or a combination of all three, she didn't care. Not anymore.

Today, Augustus had crossed a line. Today, he showed how dangerous his behavior had become. Each day the sun rose, it placed a touch more madness upon Augustus. And she wasn't going to wait to see what he did next.

She heard his footsteps approach as Duchess high-tailed it out of the kitchen. Adelia wouldn't run, and she wouldn't be nice. The time for pleasantries had passed. She would only do what was needed to get through the next few days until the doctor came to take him away.

She recalled the doctor's words about hoping it was not she that was the one creating something out of nothing all in the name of boredom. Could Augustus pull it off? Could he act sane for the duration of the doctor's visit? Her mind was already stirring up various plots in which to aggravate Augustus in subtle ways during the visit until he lost it right in front of Dr. Beeman. If that didn't work, then she would simply disappear, run away.

Easier said than done, especially on an island.

She squashed her nagging internal voice and looked directly at Augustus when he entered the room.

He treaded cautiously at first, but then increased his gait as he drew closer to her. "Adelia. Oh, my dear Adelia. What have I done?" He leaned in, trying to cup her face in his large hands. She stepped back, away from him, away from the putrid stench of alcohol.

"Don't." She held her hand up, closing her eyes. "Dinner is on the counter if you want it." She made up her own plate and settled in at the table. Never once had she failed to serve Augustus a plate; never once had he had to get off his butt and get his own dinner.

"Please. I'm so sorry. Adelia, look at me."

She lifted her head and met his gaze head-on. Were those tears? Was Augustus actually crying? So he was.

Crocodile tears, her mother used to say.

Just crocodile tears.

Her already hardened heart wouldn't allow softness for him to sneak its way in.

"I don't know how to tell you how bad I feel, how sorry I am. I'm no fool, you watered down my gin. It's the oldest trick in the book, Adelia. My own mother did it to my father. I've actually been watching for it—waiting for it."

That comment caught her attention. Seemed his father suffered at the fate of the bottle as well.

"But like my mother said to my father, it's because she loves him, and I know you did it because you love me."

Her stomach coiled at his words. Whatever love she had preserved for him vanished when he had thrown that glass at her.

But she couldn't expose her true feelings for him quite yet; for now, she would tuck her feelings deep inside of herself.

"I'll prove myself to you. I'll even wash the dishes tonight. Please give me another chance." His eyes almost, *almost* appeared as they had in those early days of their relationship. She wasn't fooled. This was a pattern for him, and she didn't trust him.

How could she love a man she couldn't trust, didn't feel safe with? One of the main reasons she had loved being with him in the beginning was because he *had* made her feel so safe.

"Eat your dinner." It was all she would give him for now. She took a small bit of delight in watching him fix his own plate and seat himself at the table. She also took some pleasure in watching him squirm as he made small talk over their meal. She merely nodded her head and continued eating. The shocker was when he stood and walked over to grab her plate. She could barely compose herself when he began washing the dishes.

Good. It was the least he could do. No amount of kindness at this point could erase his past actions. She decided to test him a bit, though.

"I think you need to stop drinking the gin." She waited him out, watching his smile turn to a neutral line, and then a frown.

"I don't think that's necessary, darling. I don't think you quite understand the life of a lighthouse keeper."

"No?"

"It's stressful in so many ways—the isolation, the monotonous work. Every day, it seems, the same tasks must be done again and again. I rise, I paint, I clean, I do, I do, I just keep doing, and it never, ever ends." He placed his head in his hands.

"It doesn't end because you won't let it. You don't need to keep repainting the walls, Augustus. Most people paint only—"

"Enough! Enough, Adelia." He slammed down his plate, water from the basin splashing over the countertops. "*I* know how to do this job, Adelia. *I* know this lighthouse inside and out. I built this house—"

She covered her ears, tears rising that she couldn't tamp down. "Stop it! I don't think I can stomach hearing this one more time. *Not one more time!*" She stood, speaking up through her ragged breath. She didn't even care what Augustus did to her; she wasn't stopping now.

"*You did not* build this house, Augustus! Samuel Gordon and his crew built this house before we even arrived on this island. *You were not* the first lighthouse keeper. Thomas Fitzgerald was. *You did not build this house, Augustus!*"

She couldn't continue; she needed to slow down her breathing. The mad spark of hysteria had risen, and all she could see was a haze of black. She felt as if she would vomit but swallowed back the bile and found her second wind. She had to finish, before he interrupted, before he silenced her.

"What about what *I* do to make this house a home? I may not paint coat over coat of needless paint over these walls. *I* don't stand there for hours at a time, staring at nothing, drinking myself to death. I *nurture* this house, try my best to make it a home, cook your meals, wash the clothes, decorate the rooms—not through blood, sweat, and tears, but through *love,* Augustus, *love!*"

He was stilled into silence, something she never thought she would see. Adelia wasn't finished. Not yet.

She walked over to the countertop where Augustus stood and took her hand from the pocket of her dress and stuck her finger straight in his face. He grabbed it, pressing down, squeezing her hand until she thought she would cry.

But she didn't.

"This isn't the house that *you* built, Augustus. This is the house that *I* built!" With a rush of adrenaline, she pulled herself from his grasp and heard the momentary madness of her words. She didn't care what she sounded like. She rushed for the door, Augustus close on her heels.

"Get back here, Adelia. You can't talk to me like that, you can't run from me."

With only fear as her guide, she raced out the door far ahead of Augustus.

CHAPTER TWENTY-ONE
1876

IT WAS AN evening like any other, yet it was to be a night that she would never forget, for it was a crucial piece of the puzzle that would ignite the course of Adelia's destiny.

Sharp, crisp wind bit at every inch of her exposed skin. Almost completely winded, Adelia spun her head once more; just to be sure she hadn't been followed here to the towering cliffs. A darkened sky matched her desperate, dismal mood.

Augustus never failed in stealing any smidgen of brightness from her mind, but tonight he had pushed until she too had crossed over the thin line to the brink of madness.

Yes—her husband was going mad.

Insane.

Insane with rage, jealously, control– sparked by boredom and gin. Adelia couldn't imagine a worse possible combination. One could activate a fire sure to burn through and destroy any soul with those caustic ingredients.

Whenever Augustus would finally place his head on the pillow beside her, Adelia would wait out the thickness, the raw stench of alcohol and bitterness, until she could finally allow herself to breathe once Augustus began to snore. It was only then that her hands would grip the quilt, which rested upon her body. Then she would cautiously count to fifty. Fifty usually did the trick, but at times she had added a few seconds more, just to be sure.

Tonight, she had run for her life, not waiting for Augustus to pass out, leaving before his before his head had even hit the pillow.

Now safely outside, her fists unclenched and her breathing slowed until she could release the soft wail that fought to escape. As if she couldn't control it, her neck craned to spy behind her once more. A momentary burst of relief washed over her until reality edged its way in once more.

She had fooled herself into thinking that if only she could try hard enough, perhaps they could get back to that sunny place where they had first fallen deeply for one another.

Was there such a spell? She frowned, knowing such a spell ceased to exist. Her trick no longer worked. She couldn't fool herself into thinking everything would be okay.

Not now.

Not anymore.

Self-reflection had once consumed Adelia. She could hardly think of anything else. At first, she wondered if their downfall could have possibly been partly her own fault. Adelia may have played a hand at her heart's demise. But, no—she had yet to find one shred of proof that argued against the fact that Augustus had been the one who had changed. Oh, it had been ever so slightly at first, an offbeat comment here and there, a sideways look. But after a few months, as surely as the dark tides shifted, it seemed that once they made the lighthouse on the cliffs their home, the very beacon which served to steer ships to safety in these treacherous waters diminished her own brightness and replaced it with a gradual shift to darkness.

She once held out a small sliver of hope that she could fix this. Yes, she had thought she could throw her shoulders back and help this stranger her husband had shifted into before it was too late.

Surely, some came back from the brink of madness, right?

The horrifying image that haunted her dreams plagued her mind once more. She shut her eyes tight, pushing the vision out of her head.

Tonight her husband had sunk to a new low, even for him.

Before the hole proved too expansive to dig out of, she told herself she needed to act—now.

Was that a shadow lurking in the distance? Was it Devon, arriving early, or had Augustus found her?

Her heart leapt with fear. No, nobody was there. It must be the wind, or possibly her mind playing tricks, for, once she focused her gaze on the spot, she could see nothing but the trees close behind her.

Adelia purposely slowed her breathing. She would need to put her plan in place quickly, but for that, she would need to speak with Devon. He should be here any minute.

But there was the sound again. This time she was sure she heard footsteps, and when she called out, nobody responded. She stood, hands clenched in tight fists, determined to face the unidentifiable figure approaching from beyond.

There was nowhere to go, of course. No choice but to

face the unknown. Adelia turned her head, her vision lit by the full moon above. She judged the distance to the edge of the cliff. There was no place else to go but down.

"Who's there? Augustus, is that you?" She spun around, her heart slamming in her chest.

Nothing.

She didn't know which direction to turn, for either way the consequences were dire if it was Augustus in the woods. Where was Devon? She needed him now, more than ever.

Wait. Straining her ears, she concentrated so hard but heard only the crickets chirping from the woods, singing their consistent nighttime melody.

She didn't move for minutes, but then finally relaxed a bit. Whatever or whomever it was, was now gone.

Her body tightened up the next time she heard it. Now she was certain; the unmistakable sound of footsteps became louder. She held her breath, ready to fight, but when she saw his face, she ran over to grab him. "I thought you'd never get here."

"I'm actually a few minutes early."

Adelia clung to him, seeking comfort as she breathed in his familiar smell; fresh and clean.

"Adelia." He moved back. "The arrangements have been made. I'm all set to leave in the morning. Once I say my final goodbye to you, I won't look back. It's going to be too hard."

"I don't want you to leave, Devon."

"I don't either, but it's the only way this can end. I can't continue to see you here on the island, I don't want to hear anything about you from other people in passing. I just want to go somewhere else, where no one knows who Adelia MacGregor is. That way, I can pretend that you don't exist."

"No, you don't understand. I want you to stay. I went to

the doctor—oh, it's a long story, but I changed my mind—about you, about us. All I need is a few more days."

"I don't understand. What happened to change your mind?" He stepped just inches closer, almost as if what she was saying didn't quite register yet. "Wait a minute. What happened to your eye?" He moved in, running his thumb carefully over her cut.

"Augustus threw a glass at me. He went into a rage." She saw the anger smoking in Devon's eyes. "He's crazy, so far gone. You're right; he's the thief. I found stolen tools under the lighthouse. But listen, I think I misunderstood the meaning of the vision. I think if I stay, he will kill me—there's no doubt in my mind."

"Oh, Adelia." He touched her as if she were made of the finest china. "I can't believe what I'm hearing. You don't know how badly I've wanted to hear those words. Is this even real?"

She could see his tears, even in the darkness. "Yes. He's beyond repair. The doctor will take him away to an asylum. I'm sure of it."

"An asylum? Isn't that a bit harsh?"

"I thought so, too. I still have reservations, but he's so ill he's become dangerous. Is there any other way?"

"That's for the doctor to decide. Let's just pray Dr. Beeman sees Augustus in his true light." Devon paused, staring at the cut on her face. "What happened tonight? I'll kill him, I swear." His finger went back to the spot underneath her eye, tracing small, light circles over the sore skin.

His touch felt good—so soothing and relaxing. She wanted to lose herself in the sensation of the protective cocoon he provided. He lifted her chin so that she would look at him. "I want to kiss you more than anything, sweet

Adelia."

She crested the pleasurable wave, giving in to the emotional pull. She wrapped her arms around him, staring into his eyes, waiting to see what his lips would finally feel like. Taste like.

"But I can't. Not yet. You're still his wife. When I do kiss you—and believe me, I will—you will be all mine."

She didn't think she could wait. Suddenly, she deflated. They had waited this long to touch each other. But now that he was close—*so close*—she was afraid if she let him go, she might never see him again, might never have a chance to kiss him. Something horrible could happen.

"What's the matter?" He took her hand and smoothed his fingers over her palm.

"It's nothing. I guess I'm a bit spooked. I just had a feeling that I'll never get to kiss you, that you'll never be mine."

"Oh, sweetheart, don't you worry about that. I'll always be here for you. Are you in danger back at the house?"

She hated to consider it, but knew that she was. "I think I am."

"Then you can't go back. I'll bring you home with me, and we'll figure out the rest in the morning. Don't worry, I'll be the perfect gentleman. You can have the bedroom, and I'll stay in the parlor."

She nodded as she listened to him, relishing the feeling of finally being safe.

"And tomorrow morning, you'll stay and cancel your boat back to the mainland?"

"Yes, I won't let you out of my sight."

"Good, Devon, good. And I'll go to Dr. Beeman's office first thing in the morning to see if he can make an emergency house call to the lighthouse."

As relieved as she was standing in the arms of Devon, it saddened her to think of what had become of her and Augustus. Not only had they failed at happiness within their marriage, but she had even botched up the job of helping him. As much as she despised what Augustus had become, she gave herself permission to mourn him; to mourn the loss of everything that was so innocent and the life she had hoped for—the children they would never have, the roots they would never lay down. Her sorrow was an anchor as she likened her feelings to grieving a death.

That's exactly what it felt like, as if Augustus had died.

Even Devon's embrace couldn't wash away the heartache that screamed and took over every inch of her being.

There it was again. The noise.

"Did you hear that?" She tightened her back.

"What?"

"That noise—listen." But she couldn't hear anything out of the ordinary now. "I just heard it."

"There's nothing there. It's just the sounds of the night settling. This can't be easy on you, but I'm here, sweet Adelia, and I'm not letting go." He rocked her, kissing the top of her head, moving to a dance as old as time.

CHAPTER TWENTY-TWO
1876

T HE NIGHT BEFORE was a blur of emotion. Waking, she gently stretched her arms overhead, yawning. Her only regret about not returning home last night was that she had left Duchess behind. Her cat was a smart girl, though, and she knew that Duchess would continue to be wary of Augustus.

Adelia walked over to the small mirror and gazed at herself, wearing Devon's nightshirt, which drifted almost to her ankles.

She wondered if Devon was still asleep or if he was waiting for her in the parlor. A stab of fear went through her as she worried about what Augustus might do once he discovered she had not come home last night. Devon would protect her, though; he had said it over and over. She trusted him, and if he made that promise, he meant every word.

A delicious scent drifted through the air, causing her stomach to rumble. Was he cooking? If she wasn't already smitten with Devon, the act of making her breakfast just might cause her to fall in love with him. Falling in love with him? Neither had spoken the words aloud.

"Devon?" she called out, walking through the parlor and into the tiny kitchen. Lately, she feared the sight of Augustus walking into the kitchen, pouring his gin. Watching Devon leaning over the woodstove to prepare a meal for her evoked emotions from her she wasn't ready to admit.

He simply stared at her for a moment, his eyes wandering over her body in his nightshirt. He cleared his throat and offered her a smile.

"I made you some tea, and your breakfast will be ready shortly." He handed her a warm, delicious smelling mug of tea. Her gaze wandered to the countertop where she saw several eggs and bread laid out.

"I could get used to all of this spoiling." She grinned, sipping at her tea.

"You have no idea what you're in for, Adelia." He kissed the top of her head. Small shivers coursed through her body as she watched him walk over to the counter.

"Did you sleep well?"

Believe it or not, she had actually gotten a wink or two of sleep, despite the stress of the last night's events. "Actually, I did."

He cracked an egg into a bowl and turned his head to speak when a sharp rapping on the door caused her to jump. Could Augustus have figured out she'd come here?

His brows creased together. "I'll be right back. Stay put."

She almost followed him to the door but decided to remain out of sight. It wouldn't be a good thing for someone from town to see her at his house, first thing in the morning, wearing his clothes.

At first, she thought the men were just talking, but then she heard Devon cry out. She ran to the window, parted the curtain, and peeked outside. From where she stood, it was difficult to see anything. She moved toward the front door, edging just out of sight. She had to get closer.

"This is crazy. Go right ahead. It's the most ridiculous thing I've ever heard!" The first thing she noticed about the two men standing there with Devon was the numerous shiny buttons adorning their uniforms.

He's in trouble.

Devon followed the men as they walked toward the back of the property. She tore over to peek out the window once more, her gaze following them as they disappeared to the back of the house. Scurrying as quickly as she could manage, she made her way to the bedroom, over to the window, and ducked out of sight on her hands and knees.

Devon's voice was the loudest, but the other men were raising their voices, too. The problem was, she couldn't figure out what they were saying because everyone shouted at once. She lifted her body just a tiny bit to peek out from behind the curtain.

Tools. Farming tools.

The scythe and the flail.

The scythe and the flail?

But that didn't make any sense—this wasn't possible. Devon made a living catching fish. He was a fisherman. He didn't farm.

Her head pounded as she thought of the tools under her house. Augustus had stolen them, she was sure of it. Why would they be here? That didn't matter right now. The only thing that mattered was setting the record straight and defending Devon.

She pounded on the window, but no one seemed to hear her. Adelia didn't consider what the officers might think of her running outside, dressed in Devon's clothes. She sprinted to the door, racing toward the commotion.

"Devon, Devon!"

The men forcibly pushed Devon, grabbing him and shoving him toward their horses.

"No! What's going on here?"

He had stopped struggling and looked at her through dejected eyes. "Go to the doctor; get there right now. And Adelia—whatever you do, don't go home."

She nodded, clutching at the nightshirt she wore, speechless. She struggled to talk, but only found her words just as they were leaving.

"Devon is not the thief. My husband is the real thief. He set Devon up, I'm telling you! I found the tools myself under the lighthouse. Stop, you have to listen to me!"

One of the men turned to face her. "Under the *lighthouse?*"

He was listening, thank God.

"Yes, my husband is the lighthouse keeper. His name is Augustus MacGregor. He's the thief; he stole the tools."

A sick chuckle erupted from the man's mouth. "I know who Augustus MacGregor is. What I don't know is why you're here with this man in his nightclothes." He swatted the backside of his horse. "Let's go."

"Adelia—do not go home!"

Clenching her fists, she could only watch as they took him away.

She was helpless to do anything but pray that somehow, some way, she could clear Devon's name and rid herself of Augustus. There was only one chance she had in succeeding, and Dr. Beeman held all the power.

"Please. I need to speak with him I beg you."

Mrs. Beeman's eyes narrowed at the sight of Adelia. She must look awful standing there, sweat and tears streaming down her face.

"My God, you're hysterical." Dr. Beeman appeared from the parlor. "What has gotten into you?" The doctor nodded to his wife and pulled Adelia from the doorway by her elbow.

"Thank you, thank you. It's Augustus. He's the thief, it's him. I found tools—a flail, a scythe. Augustus doesn't farm, he doesn't. He doesn't do anything—he just stares into space at nothing—"

"You have got to get a hold of yourself. Ellen? Please get some water, and bring it in here."

He was right. She had to calm down, otherwise he wouldn't take her seriously. "I'm sorry. I'll start over—"

"Mrs. MacGregor, I think it would be best if you just relaxed." He reached for the glass of water Mrs. Beeman had handed him.

"Yes, okay."

She took a long sip and placed it on the table. That was better.

"I'd like you to come lie down for a bit, Mrs. MacGregor."

He reached for her hand and she allowed him to lead her to the couch on the other side of the room. She took a seat and concentrated on steadying her shaking hands. He placed a pillow under her head and gently guided her down so that she was lying on the couch. After failing to calm her quaking hands, she shoved them out of sight, into the pockets of her dress.

"That's right. Now, why don't you tell me what you saw outside of Mr. Bane's home."

"What? How did you know I was there?" She bolted upright. The doctor shook his head and studied her.

"A better question would be to ask you why you were there, in Mr. Bane's nightshirt, and why you didn't sleep at your own house last night?"

How could he possibly know this? She had taken the time to get dressed and clean up a bit before coming here. Someone must have gotten here first. "How did you know that?"

"Well, when a wife fails to come home and wrongfully accuses her husband of not only going insane but of harboring stolen goods, I think it's well within a husband's rights to come looking for a doctor." He placed a hand up and down the length of her arm, attempting to soothe her, but instead, he upset her more with each stroke.

Augustus had come here? *Here?* Claiming *she* was the crazy one?

All of the pieces clicked into place. The sounds on the bluffs last night—it must have been Augustus, lurking in the shadows. My God, he would have heard every word between herself and Devon.

Everything.

No, this wasn't fair. He couldn't have the advantage here. She *had* to make the doctor believe her. She *had* to.

Her life depended on it.

Devon's life depended on it.

She looked down at the doctor stroking her arm, over and over, a frown playing on his face. Then she knew—he thought *she* was the one going mad.

"I–I'm not crazy."

"Calm down. We'll get you the help you need. Please, it's going to be okay. There're more and more experimental techniques doctors are discovering when it comes to matters of the brain."

"No!" She jumped off the couch, out of the doctor's reach. "No! I came to you first. Why are you taking his word over mine? *He's* insane. He stole the tools so that I wouldn't leave the prison that I live in!"

He didn't flinch.

"You don't believe me, do you?" She screeched the words with increasing hysteria. "Why? Because I'm a woman? Because Augustus is a man?"

"See this? You're not coherent. You're not making sense. I have to tell you, it doesn't look good from where I stand. The evidence is right there, out in the open."

Sleeping at Devon's house.

His nightshirt.

The tools in Devon's backyard.

Nothing she could say would change the doctor's mind.

She needed to run, make a break for it before they locked her up in the asylum. She realized it had become her worst fear. She was sure the officers were coming to take her away. He was stalling her, trying to keep her here.

"Mrs. MacGregor! Adelia! It's no use. They'll find you, and it really is for the best. You need help!"

She swept past the doctor's wife on the way out the door, desperately trying to think. Where was Devon? They had to be holding him. She couldn't go back to his house.

She couldn't go back to her house.

Augustus had ruined her—turned her life upside down. She pictured him, drink in hand, staring out the tower of the lighthouse, smirking. Just smirking.

Red hot revenge was the only thing on her mind as she raced through the streets, careful to take cover. They were going to lock her up. There was no way off this island. Before they did, she would make him pay. She sprinted, not taking care to avoid the mud and puddles underfoot.

Don't go back to your house.

She heard Devon's final words echoing over and over in her head, but she never was any good at taking orders.

CHAPTER TWENTY-THREE

1876

T HIS WAS IT.

Her last chance to heed Devon's words. From a distance, she stopped, gazing up at the tower. He was there—he was up there.

A flash of black streaked in front of her, and she nearly collapsed at the sight of Duchess. *Thank God.* She bent down to pet her and noticed how strangely the cat behaved. Frantically, Duchess broke free from her grasp and weaved around her legs, wailing.

"What did he do to you?" If Augustus had so much as laid a finger upon the cat, she would murder him with her own bare hands.

Duchess continued walking, back in the direction of town. She wanted to stop her, but it was best that she wasn't around for this. The cat stopped and bore her eyes into Adelia with one last wail, one last chance to join her in town, away from Augustus. Little did Duchess know that Adelia had no place left to turn, that she had nowhere to hide.

Gazing down at her wet, dirt-stained shoes, she reached down and tore both her shoes and socks off, leaving them behind in the field.

She paraded forward, her head set on exacting revenge for the countless grievances she held against Augustus. He hadn't been worthy of the title husband; he hadn't protected her, hadn't fulfilled any of her needs—not in her heart, nor her mind.

She blocked Devon's face and words from her mind, for facing Augustus, she would need to focus only on her mission at hand. With determination, she balled her fists, keeping her eyes on the tower as she marched ahead.

Augustus then did something she had never seen him do before. He turned his body in her direction, away from his beloved sea and seemed to stare right through her. As she drew closer, she was sure he was watching her, waiting for her.

Mocking her.

Taunting her.

Playing her.

Killing her slowly, one day at a time. That's what he had done best, but she was putting a stop to it.

It would end.

Today.

Opening the door to the lighthouse, Adelia stepped inside. She caught her reflection in a decorative mirror she had once lovingly hung in the foyer; taking in her haunted eyes and wild, dark hair, she barely recognized herself. With one last moment of reflection, she spied the photograph of her and Augustus on the day they had arrived on the island.

There was so much hope in their young, innocent eyes. They had such dreams for their future. The possibilities had been endless.

Don't get caught up in the past—in what will never be.

She didn't think, but acted. To keep from turning and changing her mind, she took each step, counting one by one, until, at last, she discovered that Augustus had been correct when he said there were sixty-five steps.

Sixty-five steps to her husband.

Sixty-five steps to hell.

She was turning psychotic. Right alongside her husband.

She didn't call his name. She didn't have to.

Clearly expecting her, his eyes locked with hers, and she felt his darkness, breathed his lunacy. It seeped right into her, somehow contagious. She didn't care.

It fueled her, fed her burning need, quenched her bitter thirst.

"It's your own fault."

Maniacal laughter followed; whether it came from him or her, she wasn't sure.

One.

Two.

Three.

One step. Two steps. Three steps. Four. More laughter.

She glanced down at her bare feet, wincing at the shard of glass that she had stepped on. The bastard couldn't even clean up the glass properly. His eyes held delight as her foot connected with another piece. She didn't bother to remove the glass—just kept right on walking.

They wouldn't take her away. She would rather die right here at the hands of Augustus than die a slow, creeping death at the insane asylum.

Five steps. Six steps. Seven steps. More.

Eight steps. Nine steps. Ten.

She stopped. This was it.

The end of the line, for him and for herself. She laughed, this time recognizing her own eerie cry.

No matter who killed whom, they would both be dead.

Augustus already was, and now Adelia was halfway there.

"You had to have him. You took him from me, made him your own!" He spat the words, spittle landing on her face. She didn't bother to wipe it away, just stood firmly, rooted to the top of the tower.

"You were my wife, Adelia! My wife! Devon was my only friend!" She was cognizant enough to notice he spoke in past tense.

"I'm no wife of yours, you're right about that," Adelia snarled, her hands making tight fists, digging into her exposed skin. She barely felt the blood she had created by her own hand.

"You're a joke—the both of you. Did you really think you and your *lover* could take me down? Get me carted off to an *asylum*? Oh, Adelia, how the tables have turned. Now Devon is locked up, and they're coming for you, Adelia. *You.*" His sickening laughter bellowed throughout the tower.

She didn't think, she just acted.

She rose her hand and struck him in the face, her blood-stained hands smearing traces of crimson on his cheek.

Grabbing her hand, he twisted it back until she couldn't take it. She cried out in pain, but he wouldn't let go. He persisted on turning it, squeezing. "Apologize. Apologize, Adelia, and I might consider letting you go."

Never.

He twisted harder. He was going to break her hand.

"Oh, what's the matter? Am I hurting you?" He wedged a finger from his other hand, diving his nail into the already welted flesh of her palm. "Not quite your mother's touch, but effective, all the same."

Biting down, she now saw her bare feet touching upon the honeycomb floor.

So this was it—this was what she had been waiting for.

She had learned a valuable lesson: no matter where you go, what you do, you can't change your own fate.

"Apologize!"

"Let her go!"

Devon.

Devon, Devon, Devon.

"He's nothing to us. Now apologize!"

"I'll kill you! Let her go!" Devon pounced on Augustus, but Augustus pushed back, and in the process, he released Adelia.

She tried to run, but Augustus now had Devon pinned down, right at the top of the stairs—the only way down. They struggled, the sheer madness of Augustus overpowering Devon, and there was no way he was releasing him. Augustus cackled as he strained against Devon, pushing his head down, pushing his body toward the stairs. He punched, knocking the breath from Devon, then placed his hands around Devon's neck and squeezed.

He was going to kill Devon.

If she didn't stop Augustus, he was going to kill him. She acted on sheer instinct, her own adrenaline pumping through her body, giving her strength she never knew she possessed.

Striking out at Augustus felt like the most natural thing in the world. She pushed, shoved, and punched at him, holding her own against a man almost twice her size.

"This is not the house that Augustus built—this is the house that *I built!*"

With each word, she slammed into him, harder, faster, stronger.

"I built!"

"I built!"

Devon stood, rubbing his neck, his eyes glued to the terror of the scene unfolding before him. "Adelia, that's enough! Let's go."

As if possessed by a demon, she smashed Augustus's head on the side of the railing.

Over and over and over.

All of the strength and energy had been zapped from her body, leaving her breathless, spent, and worn. Augustus lay beside her, not moving. "Don't you get it? They're coming for me. There's no hope. All I lived on these past few months, all I've wanted was hope, hope that I could survive this with a clear head, hope that I could one day be happy—maybe even with you."

"Hope?" He cocked his head. "Honey, everything will be okay, I promise."

"There's no hope—it's the only thing that kept me going. Without hope, I'm as good as dead."

"No, listen. I straightened everything out. I led the police here and they discovered more stolen goods from under the house—a lot more. They believed me. The doctor even understands. They're all outside, they'll be coming for him any minute."

"He's having me committed to an asylum." Her words failed to register.

"No, sweetheart, I spoke with the doctor. Everything is okay. They're coming to take *someone* to an asylum, but it's not you."

"It's not?" She stood, raising her blood-covered hands out to him, reaching for comfort. Devon knew her. He knew exactly what to do.

He took hold of her hand and gently traced the circles in her palm that she craved so much—the way her mother had done for many years before—smearing oval rings of scarlet, until she closed her eyes and breathed a sigh of surrender. He reached into the pocket of her dress and removed the small white stone, placing it in her hand. He understood her so well.

"Devon?" Her heart overflowed with emotion for him.

"What is it, Adelia?" He brushed her hair from her face, his eyes taking in every inch of her.

"I love you." She said the words, finally freed them from her mind. In Devon she had found a place for all her hopes. Now, it would be the two of them together. She would start over, put the horrid past behind her.

The only thing she needed now was to hear those words from his lips. She closed her eyes as Devon clasped his hands gently on hers.

"Adelia?"

She saw her world unfold in his eyes. They would become the best of friends, raise a family . . . she only needed to hear him say the words.

"Adelia!"

She saw the terror in Devon's eyes. His warning had come too late. Augustus had risen from the floor behind her, and with the last bit of his strength, twisted her to face him one last time.

She refused to let his face be the last thing she saw–instead she looked past Augustus to find hopelessness in Devon's eyes as his mouth opened wide, screaming her name, over and over.

Devon reached for her, but it was useless. Closing her eyes, she steeled herself as Augustus pushed her down, her body descending further into the depths of the long, winding staircase as her precious stone flew from her hands, out of sight. She watched her vision play out, saw her bare feet—she was helpless to stop the course of events after all.

She was going to die–right here, right now, in this house. It was *her* house and nobody could take that from her.

Her heart smashed to pieces as she mourned for Devon already and simultaneously feared for her life, knowing there truly was no hope after all. Seconds before her head hit the stairs for the final time, she saw Devon struggle as Augustus's body tumbled down, ready to suffer the same fate as her. She reached out—and tried to catch the words that she knew she would never hear from Devon's mouth.

If she had heard Devon speak the words, she could have taken them with her, for solace and comfort, to cling to forever, but instead, the last thing she heard before darkness hit were the shrill screams of Augustus.

CHAPTER TWENTY-FOUR
2017

"DEVON. DEVON BANE."

The vision hit, full force. She felt the hands of Clooney and Tracy upon her, grabbing her, attempting to soothe her, but she was lost, in another time and place. One so distant, but so near.

She saw it all this time: the bare feet in the meadow, the shadow of black fur as she glanced back.

She would not go to an asylum—nobody was putting her away.

Feeling the rage coming from deep within, she watched as the lighthouse stood before her, beckoning her to go inside and finish what needed to be done. Was she seriously going to try to take down Augustus?

This time, she knew, she understood what was happening, knew what she would find upstairs. She walked inside the foyer of the lighthouse and stopped at the antique mirror.

She closed her eyes, knowing what she would find in the reflection when she opened them, but trying to prolong the inevitable, she took just a second more to try to savor what she had found in Clooney, before she made this step.

But she also knew—knew who would be up there in a few minutes, attempting to save her. For him, she would do anything, even reenact the worst day of her life—the last day of her life.

Hope opened her eyes and sucked in a sharp breath. Her own reflection stared back at her—she took in her own tousled dark hair and her tear-stained face; gazed at her own full lips, the lips Clooney had kissed so many times.

She ran a finger over her mouth, the lips Devon had never gotten a chance to kiss.

Up, up, up.

One.

Two.

Three.

One step. Two steps. Three steps. Four. Laughter.

She glanced down at her bare feet, wincing at the shard of glass that she had stepped on. The bastard couldn't even clean up the glass properly. His eyes held delight as her foot connected with another piece. She didn't bother to remove the glass, just kept right on walking.

They wouldn't take her away—she would rather die right here at the hands of Augustus than die a slow, creeping death at the insane asylum.

Five steps. Six steps. Seven steps. More.

Eight steps. Nine steps. Ten.

She stopped. This was it.

She faced her certain demise, going through the motions of seeing, feeling everything play out just like it had the first time and a million times in her dreams. Her dreams—those repressed visions had included all of it—but she had blocked out the worst, trying to protect herself, trying to savor that last bit of hope.

Hope. She had even forgotten her real name, but she had to admit it was fitting–it was all she ever wanted but never found.

She waited until she could see Devon again. It would be any minute now. She bit back tears as Augustus twisted her bloody hand.

"Let her go!"

Devon.

Devon, Devon, Devon.

"He's nothing to us. Now apologize!"

"I'll kill you—let her go!

Standing back, Hope watched the scene unfold, taking in Devon's features, his kind eyes, wavy hair—so very similar in appearance to Clooney. It was no mystery why she and Clooney had found one another, why she held on so tightly, not wanting to lose him, not wanting to let him out of her sight. Not wanting to let him go.

But she was going to lose him too; she knew it, and no amount of denial could change what was fated to be. For now, she would savor her memory of Devon.

She tried to touch him, but the barrier of her vision and space in time prevented her from doing anything but watch. She saw herself, saw the sheer love coming, not just from her own eyes but from Devon's as well.

He took hold of her hand and gently traced the circles in her palm she craved so much—the way her mother had done for many years before—smearing oval rings of scarlet until she closed her eyes and breathed a sigh of surrender. He reached into the pocket of her dress and removed the small white stone, placing it in her hand. He understood her so well.

"Devon?" Her heart overflowed with emotion for him.

"What is it, sweet Adelia?" He brushed her hair from her face, his eyes taking in every inch of her.

"I love you." She said the words, finally freed them from her mind. In Devon she had found a place for all her hopes. Now, it would be the two of them together. She would start over, put the horrid past behind her.

The only thing she needed now was to hear those words spoken to her, from his lips. She closed her eyes as Devon clasped his hands gently in hers.

"Adelia?" She saw her world unfold in his eyes. They would become the best of friends, raise a family . . . she only needed to hear him say the words.

"Adelia!"

This was the part she couldn't stand. She covered her ears and shut her eyes, not wanting to see the look of terror on Devon's face, not wanting to see Augustus tumbling down the stairs, barreling toward her, ready to smother her with his body, his screams blending with hers, never leaving her alone—not even in death.

But then, what came next, she had never known until now. Hope heard them calling for her. She could make out the cries of Clooney and Tracy, as if from under water. She blocked them out, focusing in on the scene unfolding before her.

She had tumbled down so many stairs, too many to count. She and Augustus had laid together, separated in death by several inches.

Flashes appeared in snippets. Devon running down, holding her in his arms, sobbing recklessly, swearing as he scooped up the black cat, which had come for her after all.

Duchess. She cried out for Duchess. It had been so long since she had remembered the cat she had barely gotten to know but still had meant so much to her.

Hope listened intently to the words Devon spoke to her lifeless form.

"Don't leave me, sweet Adelia, don't go."

She heard the footsteps, knew the officers and doctor had arrived.

Hurry, Devon, hurry.

She needed to hear the words. God, after all these years, she realized it was all she had ever needed.

"No. Adelia, no." He rocked her torn, battered body, pressing his face to hers, kissing the blood, sweat, and tears from her face.

My God. Hope had heard those words, thought about those words so many times before, but now in such a different way.

The men drew closer. They called out, crying for someone to answer. Hope pressed her hands together, circling her own palm one last time as she pleaded with Devon to say those words.

"I'll never let go you, Adelia, ever. I'm sorry I failed you, but I'll love you forever." He kissed her head, howling out in pain as Duchess pressed her own body against Adelia.

"I love you, Adelia."

He said the words.

He said the words.

This entire time, she had never known, but it was true.

"I love you, too, Devon." Hope whispered the words so tenderly, reaching out, seeing the blood that was slowly beginning to drip from her hand. She turned her hand around and around, studying the blood but feeling no pain.

It was happening—she felt the shift, saw the open gashes on her hands, the blood on her feet.

Hope glanced around the room, the home she treasured so dearly, then closed her eyes once more and saw Devon laying *kisses upon her head, in another time, another realm, but time was merely a thief, stealing minutes with each tick of the clock. Time couldn't overshadow the love of the one soul she had been tied to for an eternity.*

Hope knew what she needed to do, and she also knew she should have let go such a long time ago.

"HOPE, HOPE!"

She saw the scene before her, but as she examined her blood-stained hands, she knew she had made the choice and there was no going back. She watched as Clooney clasped her lifeless, bloody hands, running his fingers across her palm, forming scarlet ovals of blood, just like his great-great-grandfather had done so many years ago. Her heart broke as she watched Clooney sobbing for her to wake up. Tracy came into focus, shaking her shoulders, gasping at the sight of the inexplicable blood, crying out to her.

She opened her mouth in an attempt to speak, but weakness overcame her. She wanted to tell them both that she loved them, but gazing up at their stricken faces, she figured they already knew.

Hope glanced around the modern kitchen, knowing now why she had never felt right in this world, why everything was such an awkward struggle.

Now she knew. She wasn't Hope after all, but a proud, confident, determined woman named Adelia who had forgotten, blocked out all of the horrors of her young life, to such an extent that her spirit had never left the grounds of the lighthouse.

The pull of the lighthouse had been inevitable, for it was where she belonged, where she stood trapped until she dealt with the events that had landed her there.

Flashes of the past years since Tracy had moved into the house flooded her. She supposed her path to the truth had begun with one of her only friends in this afterlife. It had taken a kind, trusting person such as Tracy to make Adelia feel safe enough to expose herself, she figured. The friendship that developed from there was just the beginning.

Another flash and this time she saw how everyone had seemed to look through her, from John, the owner of the pub, to the stares from the people at the bar. And Jane, the worker from the historical society. It all clicked. No wonder they had all ignored her, looked through her . . .

Every single time Adelia had been shunned passed before her eyes and a suffocating blanket lifted from her heart.

They didn't see her.

They didn't see her.

Only those people to whom she gave her trust and who played a part in her journey to closure had interacted with her, not knowing she ceased to exist to others surrounding her.

There was nothing wrong with her, she wasn't weak, she didn't need help: she was simply Adelia.

Crying out with relief centuries old, she remembered her old life—all of her friends back home, her mother, and Devon. She wept into the palm of her hands and gazed at the heavens above.

This wasn't her life anymore. As much as she loved her safe haven at the lighthouse, up on the bluffs, it wasn't where she belonged, not anymore.

Tracy would have her wedding, without Hope as her

maid of honor, but she would be fine, and Hope knew her friend would be in good hands with Tommy. Tracy had been her one true friend here in this life, besides Clooney, and for that she would be forever grateful.

What could she say about Clooney? He was Devon's relative, for sure, right down to his huge heart. If she could split her heart between the two men, she would. Clooney would make someone a fine husband one day, unlike Augustus in every single way.

Almost time. She was seconds away from leaving this world behind. Again, she tried to open her mouth to say she would miss them so terribly. But it was no use.

She would miss this place too, her beloved lighthouse; but with the sorrow of having to say a silent goodbye, there was more—so much more—waiting for her.

And then she *knew*. Knew what she had to do. It was so clear, and this time she couldn't let it slip from her mind.

"Devon…"

Clooney wept into her chest, clutching her. She needed to speak clearly so he would hear her.

This time she spoke louder, giving every bit of her effort to clear the name of the man she loved. The man who was then, now, and forever, her soul mate. She owed it to him.

She owed Devon this.

"What is it? What are you trying to tell me?" Clooney held her, his eyes fixed on hers. Tracy leaned in close, rubbing her palm.

"Devon Bane did not kill me." She knew he strained to hear her, but she gave her last bit of life to say the words again, to right a wrong.

She found her voice and this time she was sure Clooney heard every word. "Devon Bane did not kill me. My husband did–Augustus MacGregor murdered me."

She witnessed first, the confusion, and then the transformation take place in Clooney's eyes as he, too, surely fit all the pieces in place. Awe momentarily replaced sorrow in Clooney's eyes and then what he left her with was love. Sheer love. His love gave her the last bit of strength she possessed on this earth.

"Hope, don't go; don't leave me."

His sobs tore at her, but she knew there was no other way. "I love you, Clooney."

Her parting words were matched with his own, and she felt complete.

"I love you, too, Hope. I would do it all over again; I would do anything for you."

And she knew he would. He would carry out her last wish; Clooney would set the record straight for his great-great-grandfather. No longer would the rumor exist that Adelia's lover had killed her.

Her fears, her worries, her anxiety, and her agoraphobia— all of it melted away effortlessly as she succumbed to the most natural feeling in the world

For the first time in over a century, Adelia had something to look forward to. She had hope.

EPILOGUE

He had stayed on for a year. Long enough to ensure that Adelia's beloved lighthouse would have a fitting owner. Luck had it that finding a long-term lighthouse keeper was not an easy task, so the town workers had reluctantly agreed to let Devon stay on to live and work at the lighthouse until a proper replacement had come along. It ended up that Devon was reliable and skilled at the job, so he continued until he was ready to leave, even having a say about who would be hired next.

It had been bittersweet to stay on, but knowing how much she had loved the lighthouse, it was there he felt closest to her. It seemed everywhere he looked, he found some kind of reminder of her. The funny thing was, he didn't see much to remind him of Augustus.

It was her.

All Adelia.

When Adelia and Augustus had first died, Devon was never outwardly accused of the crime, although some of the officers had appeared skeptical of his innocence when he told the story of how the two had met their demise. He knew the chatter around town that circulated about the topic as well. People could think what they want. They had been doing it for centuries and would continue to do so, long after he passed as well.

Only Devon knew the awful truth and how Augustus had finally succumbed to his fate that day. It was something he would not discuss with anyone, not since he uttered the last word about Adelia and Augustus to the officers.

At times, he could have sworn he saw a shadow lingering, an unexplained noise from the stairway, and he would have bet from the way Duchess behaved at times that she had witnessed things, too. But then, he realized it had most likely been wishful thinking on his part, for he would have given anything to secure a tie with Adelia.

When he had finally found a young couple to pass the lighthouse along to, he wished them the best, hoping they had better luck here than Adelia and Augustus had. He had stood on the property the day he left, suitcase and Duchess in hand, peering up at the tower of the lighthouse.

Adelia's lighthouse. He would always remember it that way.

There was no place left for him on the island. It was time to move on, time to find a suitable home and get on with this life. As a skilled fisherman, he would find work elsewhere. Before the night that had solidified Adelia's fate, he had planned to head south, somewhere in New York, perhaps, maybe close to the city.

One thing remained constant—wherever Devon lived

and whomever he surrounded himself with, Adelia never wandered far from his mind.

When he finally settled into a small town in New York, he and Duchess found a charming saltbox home and although the yard bordered on a cemetery, it never spooked him.

He continued to make his living as a fisherman by the river formerly know as North River, now known as the Hudson River.

As he sat in his yard one day, a glass of lemonade in hand, he recalled memories of Adelia, and instead of feeling sad, he felt blessed to have known her.

Duchess scampered over to the stone house next door where her favorite playmate, a little girl named Lillie, lived. He chuckled as he watched Lillie scoop Duchess in her arms, attempting to teach Duchess how to play potsie on the dirt lot. Devon continued to watch as Lillie threw a rock and then jumped the squares of the board etched into the dirt with a stick.

It was the little things he enjoyed lately; they filled up his life. So far, he hadn't found anyone to capture the attention of his heart, and he knew the fact that Adelia resided there might be part of the problem.

Maybe someday.

Maybe not.

Either way, Devon knew that he and Adelia would eventually find their way to back to one another.

THE END

ACKNOWLEDGEMENTS

As a writer, I love when ideas come to me from the setting of places I've had the pleasure of visiting. Amity Island is a fictional island I created, based on many beautiful seaside towns, which have inspired me to create Adelia's unique story.

Thank you to my amazing family. Mom, Dad, Alexandra, Alan, Jimmer, Damian, Amanda, and Siobhan—thank you for your continued love and support.

Thanks to all of my friends and a special mention to my longtime friends for many, many years of friendship and love—Janine, Jen, Jim, Karen, and Kim.

A big shout out to my street team; thank you for your help promoting and beta reading all of my novels and providing valuable feedback. Dawn Yacovetta, thanks again for the all of the wonderful feedback, I truly appreciate all you do.

Kathleen Payne, you are a lifesaver! I can't say thank you enough for all of your wonderful input and ideas.

Jena Brignola, thank you for the beautiful cover once again. You've captured the essence of Adelia perfectly.

Jill Sava, thank you so much for your help formatting, it's always great working with you.

Sara Meadows, thanks so much for all of your hard work as my editor and PA, and of course for your friendship.

Lastly, I would like to thank my readers, there's nothing like sharing my stories with you and hearing your valuable feedback. I hope you love reading Adelia's story as much as I enjoyed writing it.

You can follow me at:
www.myaomalley.com
Instagram @myaomalley
Facebook.com/myaomalley

XOXO
Mya